"I'm worn out," Rio grumbled. **"Can we just get the rest of my clothes on so I can go to sleep?"**

Binney tucked the single crutch under his bare arm and slipped her arm around his damp waist. "I'll be quick."

It took them a while to make it across to the bed, where Rio sank back with a groan.

Binney was totally unprepared to experience a punch in her gut from merely looking at him sprawled on his bed in nothing but briefs. Averting her eyes, she started at his feet and worked up his legs, and felt his suspicious gaze track her every move.

Privately she chanted, *You're a nurse. He's a patient. You're a nurse. He's a patient.*

One fine-looking patient who showed by his grin that he'd begun to enjoy the whole process way too much as she smoothed lotion over his chest and the nicely rippled muscles along his lower abs.

A BABY ON
HIS DOORSTEP

BY
ROZ DENNY FOX

MILLS & BOON

First Published in Great Britain 2017
By Mills & Boon, an imprint of HarperCollins*Publishers*
1 London Bridge Street, London, SE1 9GF

© 2017 Rosaline Fox

ISBN: 978-0-263-92310-0

23-0617

Our policy is to use papers that are natural, renewable and recyclable products and made from wood grown in sustainable forests. The logging and manufacturing processes conform to the legal environmental regulations of the country of origin.

Printed and bound in Spain
by CPI, Barcelona

Roz Denny Fox's first book was published by Mills & Boon in 1990. She writes for several Mills & Boon lines and her books are published worldwide in a number of languages. Roz's warm home-and-family-focused love stories have been nominated for various industry awards, including the Romance Writers of America's RITA® Award, the Holt Medallion, the Golden Quill and others. Roz has been a member of the Romance Writers of America since 1987 and is currently a member of Tucson's Saguaro Romance Writers, where she has received the Barbara Award for outstanding chapter service. In 2013 Roz received her fifty-book pin from Mills & Boon. Readers can email her through Facebook or at rdfox@cox.net, or visit her website at www.korynna.com/rozfox.

I'd like to dedicate this story to my daughters
and their families. You make me so proud,
and you complete my life.

Chapter One

Rio McNabb vaguely registered the sights, sounds and blended odors of hay, animals and concession stands at the regional rodeo in Abilene, Texas. Really he'd honed in more on the bronc rider who preceded him who'd failed to make the required time to be in money contention.

Striding toward his chute, he smiled at the handlers preparing the mount that would be his last ride with the PRCA. He'd earned enough over his years on the Professional Rodeo Cowboys Association circuit to buy the Lonesome Road Ranch from his folks. Like most ranchers they'd been land rich and cash-strapped. But after today he could cut back rodeos and concentrate on building his horse-breeding business. The ranch, situated well off any beaten path, was a secluded spot where he and his twin brother were third-generation McNabbs born and raised there. Not that Ryder cared, although maybe someday he'd change his mind. Championships meant far more to him than they ever had to Rio.

Having traveled across the States since junior rodeos, he'd be glad to get off the road. Several years ago his parents had sold all of their cattle to happily retire at a senior living complex in San Antonio. At the moment they were on their dream vacation in Australia.

Bronc riding had been good to him, though. A win today would be a fine way to go out, plus give him more than enough funds to buy a palomino mare he'd had his eye on for a while.

All at once he heard a commotion in the chute. The bronc he'd drawn to ride today, Diablo Colorado, Spanish for Red Devil, was new to the circuit. Rio had given him a cursory inspection earlier and noted the horse was a big, powerful sorrel gelding. Rio guessed the animal was living up to his name based on the difficulty handlers were having getting him into the chute.

"Don't envy you this one," Colton Brooks called down to Rio.

He smiled and acknowledged the warning, although feisty horses weren't anything new to him. Over the years he'd suffered his share of hard knocks, bruises and even a few broken bones. Probably another reason at thirty-two to hang up his spurs and leave serious competition to the young dudes. Unlike his brother, a hypercompetitive bull rider who reveled in piling up points in his sport to be acclaimed in the professional standings, Rio had been content to seek out smaller venues with fair winnings. Rather than sticking with the PRCA, he figured after today to keep his hand in by joining the RHAA. The Ranch

Horse Association of America showcased skills of true cowboys. His twin scoffed at those events, and at the notion of ever returning to the homeplace Ryder called Hicksville Ranch. Thinking about that had Rio grimacing. He loved the Lonesome Road and would be happy to live there until he couldn't climb aboard a horse anymore.

Tightening his gloves, he resettled his dove-gray Stetson before climbing up to join the handlers who'd finally gotten Diablo into the chute.

Rio sank onto the saddle, then vaulted out again as the horse bucked inside the enclosure and wildly tossed his head. Rio considered asking for a tie line to run from the bit to the cinch. A head-tosser could easily break a rider's nose, or blacken his eyes. But hearing the crowd cheer and chant his name, and because he alone knew this was his goodbye ride, he decided to ride this devil and give the fans their money's worth.

Gingerly taking his seat again, Rio wrapped the reins tight, slid his boots into the stirrups, raised his right arm and let out a rebel yell.

The gate slammed open. The sorrel bucked stiff-legged right in the opening. And instead of bolting or bucking into the larger arena, Diablo rose on his hind legs and without warning crashed over backward, crushing Rio between seven hundred fifty pounds of muscled horse and a well-built, steel-reinforced wooden fence that he felt crack around him.

Even as he tried to haul in a deep breath, Rio heard a collective "oh" roar from the crowd. There was a momentary cacophony of curses amid fast-shuffling booted feet, seconds before everything in his world went black.

The strident sound of sirens awakened Rio to the urgent shout of old Doc Kane, a much-appreciated rodeo doctor. Rio tried to ask a question, but pain battering him from all sides seemed to clamp a fist around his voice box.

Doc called for morphine, and before Rio could object he felt the sharp sting of a needle entering his thigh and he was lost in oblivion again.

Rio opened his eyes, but didn't recognize anything around him. He felt weighted down in a sea of white. Odd beeps came from somewhere overhead. Two men, both blurs of ocean blue, bent over him. He tried to move to see around them, but couldn't seem to do that. He felt his heart begin to pound as panic set in.

"Dr. Layton, he's awake." The figure at Rio's left shined a bright penlight in each of his eyes.

Blinking, Rio attempted to sit up. A heavy hand pressed him down. Excruciating pain followed. Enough to have him gritting his teeth.

"Settle down, son. I'm Arthur Layton, chief of general surgery at City Hospital. This is Dr. Mason, our surgical resident. A horse fell on you at the rodeo. You're not long out of surgery and still in pretty bad shape."

"Is the horse okay?" Rio croaked. He began to remember bits and pieces, like seeing the chute open, feeling Diablo rear right before something went terribly wrong.

"You're worried about the horse?" The surgery chief snorted. "Worry about yourself, Mr. McNabb. I'm afraid your rodeo days are over. You broke your clavicle, cracked two thoracic vertebrae we may still later need to stabilize. You have a fractured left wrist and badly sprained right ankle. Oh, and there was the pneumothorax we hope stays fixed."

Surfacing through the pain, Rio licked dry lips. "A pneumo what? What is that?"

"Collapsed lung," the resident supplied.

The older doctor unwound his stethoscope, listened to Rio's chest, then typed on his computer. "We inserted a chest tube to reinflate your left lung. It still sounds good. We'll keep a close eye on it, though. I've ordered pain meds as needed. With luck, by next week we can move you from ICU into a ward."

"I can't stay here," Rio said. "I've gotta get to my ranch." For one thing, he was seeing dollar signs for all this surgery stuff.

Dr. Layton's voice gentled. "According to some of our nurses you're famous. I know performing in the rodeos makes you tough, but I can't release you until you're able to get up and around. You don't have a fractured skull, but you shook your brain."

"Famous? Not me. They must mean my twin, the bull-riding champion." Rio tried again to scoot up in bed, but yelped when pain gripped him.

Scrolling through Rio's computer chart, Layton frowned. "I figured you'd have someone at your ranch to cook and clean. But I see the last time you were seen here for a concussion you signed yourself out against staff's advice. This states you're single. If that's still the case, who'll care for you at home?"

"I'll take care of myself," Rio growled. "Health insurance companies don't like guys in my line of work. Paying my bills depends on me getting home to help my only ranch hand ready our colts and fillies to sell."

The doctor shook his head. "Sorry," he said, closing out the document and tapping the hand Rio didn't have in a cast. "You're in serious shape, son. My best estimate is you'll be six months recovering to a point where you can take care of your ranch. From here you'll go to a rehabilitation facility where you'll have therapy to regain strength."

Rio tried to shake his head but was stopped by the tight neck collar. Clenching his jaw, he said, "No. Rehab isn't an option. Where's my cell phone? I need to call JJ, my ranch hand, to collect my pickup and camper from the rodeo grounds. I left my dog, Tag, in the unit while I went off to ride. JJ can look after our horses, but running the ranch is my responsibility." He managed to gesture with the hand not in a cast, but discovered that arm was tangled up with IV lines.

"I don't think you get it, McNabb. For a while you're going to require assistance getting in and out of bed, to and from the toilet and shower, and fixing food. Maybe Lola Vickers can come out of retirement to take on a private duty nursing assignment," the doctor mused aloud.

The resident interrupted. "This morning I noticed Binney Taylor on the ER roster. Must mean she finished her private duty job for Bob Foster's wife."

"Binney would see he keeps his braces and casts from getting wet. I suppose she can cook or she wouldn't have lasted caring for Raenell Foster. Is Binney strong enough to keep this guy from falling and taking her down with him? It'll be some time before he regains good balance. I still say rehab's the best place for him."

Rio scowled. "I'm not going to any damned rehab. You're saying I could get a nurse to come out to the ranch?"

"Yes. A private duty nurse boards on-site for a set amount of time. Not cheap, but may be less expensive than the cost of being in rehab. A home nurse can handle initial physical therapy and see that you get to follow-up appointments here."

The resident went to a cabinet, opened a drawer and pulled out a business card he passed to the surgeon. "You could give Binney a call and see if she's available."

Layton took out his phone. He punched in a number then handed Rio the card. "Binney, Dr. Layton at City General," he said into the phone. "Steve Mason tells me you've ended your assignment at the Foster ranch." He listened a moment. "Uh-huh. Well, I've a possible new client. A local rodeo cowboy who's been banged up pretty bad." Grimacing, the doctor said plainly enough, "Rio McNabb has a stubborn streak a mile wide. I've no doubt he'll be a handful. Before you agree to take the job I recommend dropping by ICU to talk with him. I know Lola swore she's retired for good, but possibly you can twist her arm to take this one. She'd give back any guff she's handed." He listened again. "Okay, I'll tell him."

Layton clicked off his phone. "She heard about your accident on the news. Apparently you two went to high school together. Today she works a three-to-eleven shift in our ER, so can swing by around two. That way you can ask any questions you may have." Finished speaking to Rio, the doctor waited until Rio said grouchily that he'd talk to the nurse, but added that he didn't recall knowing her. "My ranch hand is older than me. He may know her. I'll ask him as soon as I get my phone back."

The two doctors stepped aside as a gray-haired nurse bustled into the room. "I have Mr. McNabb's pain shot."

Dr. Layton nodded, then said to Rio, "Either I or Dr. Mason will be back to check your breathing around supper time. This is Nurse Murphy. Do what she says. Say, Murph, Mr. McNabb wants his phone. Is it among his personal effects you've put somewhere?"

She went to a cabinet and took out a sack with a list stapled to the front. "Yes, we have his cell. I'll let him make a call while I record his vitals. This pain med you ordered will send him nighty-night."

Shrugging at each other the doctors left the room.

Rio took his phone and with some difficulty called JJ Montoya. "JJ, it's Rio. I'm stuck in City Hospital. Will you ask Rhonda to take you to pick up my truck and camper from the rodeo grounds? I left Tag while I rode."

"I'm ahead of you, Rio. Rhonda already drove me over there, and I brought your rig home."

"You did? Is Tagalong okay?" Rio had been worried about the ginger-colored stray dog that had found him a couple of years ago in the Mesquite Rodeo parking lot. His vet had called the stray an Australian Labradoodle. To Rio the big mutt was simply a great companion on lonely treks between rodeos.

"Tag's fine. How are you?"

"Docs say I'm pretty stove-up, JJ." He listed the injuries Layton had named. "Say, will you check on the bronc that dumped me into the fence? His name's Diablo Colorado. He's from Weldon Walker's rodeo string."

"I ran into Colton Brooks. He said a vet checked the horse. He may have fared better than you. Only had a few scrapes."

"I'm thankful he didn't break a leg and have to be put down. Not that I envy the next rider who draws him," Rio mumbled. "But this was his first rodeo. You know, JJ, I'd decided that ride would be my last in the PRCA. The surgeon says it'll likely be my last bronc ride anywhere."

"What do doctors know about cowboy grit? You've been banged up before and have healed fine."

"I hope you're right and he's wrong." He glanced up at the nurse who had finished recording his temperature and pulse. "Listen, there's a nurse here with pain medication, and I'm starting to think I should take it. I'm, uh, not going to be able to help wean and train our young stock the rest of this year. We can talk about hiring you part-time help once I'm home." The two men signed off and Rio let the phone fall to his side. That was when he realized he'd forgotten to ask if JJ knew a Binney Taylor.

"I'll set the phone on your tray table," Nurse Murphy said. After doing so she took the cap off a syringe, swabbed Rio's upper arm and administered the drug.

"Don't they have pain pills? I hate sh-shlots," he muttered. But clearly his ability to speak was already compromised.

AT TWO O'CLOCK, after donning a sterile gown, booties and gloves, Binney Taylor entered the ICU room where Rio McNabb lay trussed up like a Christmas goose. She could hear the soft whiffle of a snore indicating her arrival hadn't wakened him. And that was good. It gave her time to collect her thoughts at seeing him in person again.

In high school the popular and handsome McNabb twins were crushed on by every girl in school, including her. As someone who didn't travel in their sphere, she'd been particularly drawn to Ryder McNabb and had loved him from afar. Then in her junior year, Ryder had asked her to the spring dance.

Beyond thrilled she'd borrowed a nice dress and then spent money she didn't have to spare on having her hair done. And she'd arranged for a night off from her after-school job. Ryder never showed up to collect her at the group home. Nor had he called. Later it'd been cruelly pointed out by mean girls at school that he'd taken Samantha Walker to the dance. He had never bothered to apologize, and the rejection lingered until she got to nursing school, where in time she'd learned to value her self-worth.

She hadn't run into either twin since they graduated from high school the year before her. She knew they were both following the rodeo. As she gazed at Rio, she was transported back to a time when the very thought of administering care to either of the hot, popular twins would've left her feeling awkward. Now Rio McNabb was just another unlucky cowboy in need of nursing.

Binney opened his computer chart with her access card. Reading over the many injuries diagnosed in ER, her empathy for him grew. His recovery was going to be arduous. It was easy to see why Dr. Layton thought she might hesitate being stuck on such a remote ranch, forced to ride herd on someone the surgeon had indicated could be cantankerous. But she was well trained and good nurses handled all types of grumpy patients.

She closed out of his record, and glanced up to find the patient in question studying her with serious gray eyes.

"If you're here to deliver another shot for pain,

forget it. I don't like how they knock me out. I can't recover if all I do is sleep my life away. And tell that hospital advocate who came by to say I need to book an ambulance to take me home next Saturday, and rent a hospital bed for a month or so, that the wrangler who works for me will collect me in his pickup. No one's gonna turn me into an invalid."

"Actually, I'm not on your nursing team. Dr. Layton said he told you I'd drop by around two today so we could talk about your home care. I'm Binney Taylor, a private duty nurse. I see you don't remember me. We attended the same high school. You and your brother graduated a year prior to me."

"You're a home nurse? You look so young," he blurted. "Layton said we went to the same high school, but I assumed he meant you went there years before me."

"I believe age is just a number. But if you have questions as to whether or not I'm competent," she said testily, "I can provide you with references."

"Sorry. I suppose you're capable. High school was a long time ago for both of us. To be truthful, I don't remember you." He closed his eyes. "The shots they give me mess with my head. I wake up fuzzy. I don't like it, not thinking clearly, I mean."

Frankly it irritated her to hear so bluntly that she was totally forgettable, although it shouldn't surprise her. Back then all kids who lived in the group home were made fun of by cliques of their popular peers. That didn't mean she had to endure his slights now.

Taking out her cell phone, she phoned Lola Vickers, the former private duty nurse. "Hi, Lola, it's Binney. Dr. Layton has a patient at City who's going to need home care in a week or so. Can you take this job?"

"No. Arthur called me. I'm retired. My husband and I plan to travel. Why can't they get that through their heads?"

"Oh, I didn't know Dr. Layton had contacted you. Sorry." She chewed the corner of her lower lip and eyed the man in the bed. "I know you turned the area over to me, Lola. I am free to take this assignment. It's more that this patient wants a nurse with more experience. But I understand. Enjoy your trip. I'll talk to you later. Bye."

Rio glared. "Did I question your experience? I just don't want anybody caring for me at my ranch." He rubbed the furrows that'd formed between his eyebrows. "Can you cut me some slack? I feel like I'm navigating through fog."

Binney reopened his record. "I see you are on a heavy-duty opioid. Are you aware that you sustained serious injuries? While you're here you should let them do whatever they can to keep you pain-free. Really, though, I am happy to hear you'd rather not take painkillers. Once you get home and settled we can certainly start cutting back." Jerking upright, she keyed out and guiltily met his searing gaze. "Uh, that's providing you elect to hire me. I didn't mean to be pushy. Dr. Layton called Lola Vickers, but she's not available."

"Do I need to decide right now? I've been tossed

off horses before, and even been kicked in the head. After those docs patched me up I recuperated on my own at the ranch. Anyway, the Lonesome Road, my ranch, is well named. It's two hundred acres in the middle of nowhere." He gestured with his hand and once again the IV lines rattled. "Someone like you would get bored there before a day passed."

She began backing toward the door. Seeing the shape he was in she probably shouldn't take personally his reluctance to hire her. After she'd taken over from Lola as the only private duty nurse in the ranch community around Abilene, her jobs were mostly caring for ranchers or their wives following simple surgeries. There was Tom Parker, who'd been gored by a bull and gangrene had set in. Besides nursing she'd done their cooking so Tom's wife could get their cattle to market. She could handle McNabb's job.

To be honest she felt rattled over the possibility of working for the fancied McNabb brother. Someone who had matured and had definitely gotten more muscular. Even amid all his casts and bandages, and with the scruff of a five o'clock shadow, Rio McNabb was still handsome as sin. Had he become better looking than Ryder? The deeper question—was he nicer?

Quickly contemplating what it'd be like to share his home if it was as remote as he indicated, all while handling his most intimate needs, left her thinking this was probably a bad idea.

She was almost out the door when Rio called, "Hey. In high school, did you date my brother?"

The pain caused by that query even so many years later sent Binney spiraling in anger. But, loath to admit that his brother had stood her up, she stepped fully into the room again. "Are you kidding? I never garnered Ryder's attention, although it wasn't for the lack of my hoping to."

Rio might have responded, but Nurse Murphy came into the room and stopped to greet Binney. "Hey, hello. How's Raenell Foster? I heard you were taking care of her after her heart attack. What a shock. She's my age, you know. And she was never an ounce overweight. Nothing like me," the woman said, patting her ample girth.

"I completed my stint at the Fosters'." Binney glanced at her watch. "In fact I'm filling a few shifts in ER until another outside job comes up. I'm working three to eleven tonight. Guess I'd better go grab the elevator to keep from clocking in late." She dredged up a smile for Rio then peeled off the sterile gloves and gown she'd donned to enter ICU.

Gertrude Murphy shot a furtive glance between her patient and Binney. "Oh, so you two are friends." She broke into a wide smile. "Or more than friends? I forget you younger nurses have lives outside of the hospital. If you two are dating, feel free to stop back anytime."

Binney choked. "We're not friends. Dr. Layton thought Mr. McNabb might have need of home nursing once he's dismissed from here." She wadded up her used gown. "He doesn't think he'll require home care."

"Of course he will." Gertrude made a face. "Wait'll the morphine wears off and we try to get him up to see if he can manage crutches. The tougher these cowboys are, the harder they go down. You'd better keep in touch."

"I'm not deaf," Rio exclaimed, gray eyes thunderous. "And I don't think I said for sure I wouldn't need help, only that I didn't want it. Dr. Layton or the resident said they'd be back to check me this evening. Earlier I wasn't thinking straight. Now I have some definite questions for the doctor as to my prognosis. So, Binney...er, Nurse Taylor, keep in touch, okay?"

She felt a childish urge to stick her tongue out at him. Instead she inclined her head, and murmured to Gertrude, "The hospital has my phone number and ER schedule." With that, she spun away, dumping everything in the trash receptacle situated right outside his room.

"It doesn't sound as if you made a very good impression," Gertrude chided, marching to Rio's bedside.

He scowled all the way through her taking and logging in his vital signs. He practically growled when she pulled a syringe from the deep pocket of her uniform. "No more shots for pain."

"Dr. Layton ordered a shot every three hours through tomorrow. Then he'll reevaluate."

"The stuff you give me knocks me out cold."

She grinned. "That's the point. Sleep facilitates

healing. Come on. Don't make me call in an orderly to hold you down."

Rio noticed pain had begun to seep back. "Is there a reason I need to sleep sitting up?"

"You had a collapsed lung. You don't want it deflating. I expect if all sounds good later, your surgeon will give us leeway to adjust the head of your bed. Between a tightly taped clavicle, a neck brace and recovering from a pneumothorax, sleeping reclined for the time being is preferable. Has anyone suggested you order a hospital bed to use at home?"

"Yes." His scowl deepened.

"So is that what you and Binney were fussing at each other about?"

"Were we fussing?" Rio didn't care to tell a friend of Nurse Taylor's that his irritation at the younger nurse centered on the fact she'd all but admitted to lusting after Ryder. Not that he wasn't used to women flocking around his more flamboyant twin, like bees buzzing over a flowerpot. He wondered when it had started bothering him so much. Possibly when he heard admiration for his twin falling from the kissable lips of the attractive blonde nurse with the striking green eyes. Those eyes were memorable, and yet he couldn't place her. Damn!

Since his head had cleared a little, he searched his memory bank back to high school. It annoyed Rio that he continued to draw a blank when it came to Binney Taylor. He could phone Ryder on the PBR circuit and run her name by him. Given their last falling out, he quashed that thought. JJ was a bit older, but he might remember Binney Taylor. Or his fiancée, Rhonda, who'd also attended their high school.

Why did any of this matter? Why waste time worrying about the past when he didn't even want to hire a private duty nurse?

In spite of telling himself that, Rio was beset by a longing to see her again. As he tried to sort through why that was, Nurse Murphy popped him with the needle she brandished, and in seconds Rio slipped out of the real world again.

Chapter Two

A bright light blinding Rio in one eye ejected him from a dark stupor. He tried to move his head to get away from the light, but was hamstrung by an immovable plastic collar he vaguely remembered someone clamping around his neck. His opposite wrist and ankle hurt like the devil when he moved either one, so he lay still until he could get his bearings.

"You are still alive," Dr. Layton said, shutting off the penlight as he continued to loom above Rio.

Devoid of words, Rio simply blinked. Ever so slowly his thoughts coalesced with his body. "Barely alive," he finally got out.

"Did you insult one of our nurses?" Layton pulled up a stool and sat next to Rio's upper torso. He unhooked his stethoscope and plugged in one ear tip, all the while checking Rio's pulse.

"If I did it's probably because you're doping me up like some street junkie," Rio managed to feebly say. "I don't recall insulting Nurse Murphy. But I didn't mince words objecting to that last pain shot. I can't remember what happens after one of those."

"So I've heard from a few staff members. Including from one who claimed she couldn't wake you to eat the soup I ordered for your supper." The doctor clamped in his other ear tip and slid the metal chest piece over Rio's lungs and diaphragm. After he finished listening, he sat back and slung it around his neck. "Both lungs are getting good air. Any chest pain now will be from the vertebrae and clavicle. You're lucky you have strong ribs. A broken rib on top of everything else would've added months to your recovery."

"Lucky. Yeah, that's me." Rio wrinkled his nose and tried to scoot up in bed, but couldn't get any traction between his hand being in a cast and his opposite ankle in an inflatable one that extended below his heel.

"We need to try and get you up. I'll have our orthopedic man on staff drop by and see if the swelling in your ankle is down enough to exchange the temporary cast for an Ace wrap. That should give you some better mobility. How's the rest of your pain?"

"Manageable, I think. I guess I don't really know since I'm zoned out more than I'm awake. Out of curiosity, who did I insult? If I swore at one of the nurses, I'm sorry."

"Nothing that bad. You apparently have issues with Nurse Taylor. Whatever transpired between you two gave her second thoughts about working for you. Since Lola Vickers opted out, you'd best get used to the idea of spending a few weeks at Baxter Rehab."

After typing on Rio's chart, the doctor then clicked off the system and rose.

Rio's main issue with Binney Taylor was that she looked like a model, and in her own words once, and maybe still, harbored a desire for his brother. But were either of those things reasons for him to dismiss her services? Hell's sake, he didn't want to spend weeks away from his ranch.

"To tell you the truth, Doc, my conversation with Nurse Taylor isn't totally clear. Could you apologize for me and ask her to come back to talk again?"

"I can do that." Layton glanced at his watch. "In fact, she's due to clock out of ER in a few minutes. I want someone to get you up to see if you can stand with crutches, and with help walk a few steps. The night duty nurse will check your vital signs, but if Binney's available, let's see if she can assist you out of bed. We'll be more inclined to release you to go home if the two of you manage walking. Provided she'll take you on as a private patient."

The doctor talked so fast Rio had difficulty processing everything. Enough registered for him to know he needed to be on his best behavior with Nurse Taylor. Really he just needed to satisfy Dr. Layton. Once he got home what would hold him to keeping a private duty nurse? Couldn't he tell her he no longer required her help? What was most important was for him to go home, where, even if he was housebound, he'd be there to confer with JJ and do the ranch bookkeeping and such.

A nurse Rio didn't remember meeting bustled

in to remove the inflatable cast and rebandage his ankle. Her badge said her name was Janet Valenzuela. In the course of their short conversation she revealed that she knew JJ and Rhonda. "I watched you ride in last year's Abilene rodeo," she said as she attached the clips to hold Rio's Ace bandage in place. "My son and a friend do team roping."

"Would that be Carlos? If so, I know him. He and his partner are moving up in PRCA standings. Even before the accident this was going to be my last circuit ride. I did think I'd sometimes enter ranch rodeos." He tried to move his newly taped ankle. Pain shot up his leg and made him catch his breath. "Plainly that won't be for a while," he said through compressed lips.

About that time Dr. Layton walked back into the room accompanied by Binney Taylor. They both heard his last exchange.

"Working here the last fifteen years I've met a lot of you stubborn rancher and rodeo types," the doctor said. "I've seen a few who don't take my professional medical advice end up in the obit column of the local paper. You can be one of them, Rio, or you can follow my orders and be content raising and selling horses. Barring being caught in a tornado, you could live happily into old age."

Rio caught Binney and Janet both wincing at the doctor's blunt statement. Because his previously addled brain was beginning to connect to the truth of his situation, Rio thought he could accept Dr. Layton's advice. "Some rodeo jocks don't have options. I'm lucky to have the ranch as a fallback." Rio mustered a smile. "Earlier I may have sounded like a blockhead. I understand my life has drastically changed. Truly I'm not like some guys who see rodeo as their whole life. I have a twin like that," he added, his gaze boring into Binney as he spoke.

"You act as if that's significant to me," she replied. "Until today I hadn't seen you or Ryder since the night of your high school graduation, when, as a junior, I helped set out snacks. You both went on the all-night party. I worked two jobs all through high school. That's how I paid for nursing school. Which reminds me," she said, handing him a manila folder, "as I'm the only private duty nurse currently in the area, here's a copy of my nursing diploma and recommendations from nursing professors. The hospital HR had them on file. If you'd like I can get references from my private duty jobs over the past two years."

"We're wasting time," Dr. Layton said. "I'm vouching for you, Binney. This guy has two choices, go to Baxter Rehab or hire you. Without further ado, can you ladies help our patient out of bed? Janet, I ordered crutches for him. Will you see if they were delivered to the nursing station?"

Acknowledging the doctor with a nod, the older nurse hurried from the room.

RESOLVING TO MAKE this work for Rio's sake, Binney slid her arm behind his back to give him support so he could ease his injured torso off the pillows. When her hand accidentally burrowed between his loosely tied hospital gown and the naked flesh of his muscular back, she and Rio both sucked in shocked breaths.

"Sorry about my cold hand," she hastily mumbled. "My bad. But someone needs to tie your gown tighter. It's only loosely done up at the top."

Having quickly jerked back fingers that still tingled from touching him, Binney made sure to have cotton fabric between her hand and Rio's smooth, warm back during the next attempt to sit him up. *Her reaction made no sense.* She was, after all, trained to see bodies as machines. In all her seven years as a registered nurse caring for young, old and in-between men and women of all shapes and sizes, she didn't remember ever having experienced such an immediate visceral reaction to simply touching anyone's skin.

A nursing aide entered the room carrying a set of adjustable crutches. "Janet got called to a patient having problems in another room. She said she may be a while."

The surgeon huffed out an irritated sigh. "I could help you, Binney. But the object is to see if you can get him out of bed."

"I'll manage. Are the crutches set for someone Rio's height?"

Dr. Layton took them from the aide, who quickly retreated. "I'm six-one and he's about the same. These would work for me. Just see if you can help him stand, Binney. I'll save ordering him trying to walk until tomorrow."

Not in the habit of arguing with attending physicians, nevertheless Binney knew it would be a disappointment for Rio to have walking put off. He'd made plain earlier how he resented feeling like an invalid.

Lowering her voice, but speaking directly to him, she said, "This will be awkward considering you have injuries to both sides of your body. Might I suggest you try using one crutch? The one opposite your usable foot. Let me act as the stabilizer for your right side. I can keep you upright and guide the portable infusion hanger, while you sort of hop along on your good leg."

"That's risky," the doctor said. "He must outweigh you by fifty pounds, and could bowl you right over."

"I'm five-eight and stronger than I look." Binney smiled encouragingly at Rio.

"All right. I'll be here this time to catch any slip." Dr. Layton walked over and passed Rio one crutch.

"Dang. The cast makes it hard to grip the handhold," Rio muttered. "Are you sure you want to try bearing my weight?" he asked Binney, who'd settled his right arm over her shoulder, and this time had her arm firmly around his waist as she slid him to the edge of the bed.

"Trust me," she murmured near his ear.

TOTALLY CAUGHT OFF guard by the force of tremors running from his toes to his head as he experienced her touch and warm breath at his ear, Rio tested his uninjured foot on the floor and stood. Determined he could do this, he nevertheless needed a moment to get used to the feel of Binney's soft breast and other womanly curves pressed tight into his side and hip.

"I've got you," she said in a sure voice from somewhere in the vicinity of his chin. "I know you want to use the bathroom. It's about twenty steps to get you there. Are you game to try?"

Rio felt cool air from the room's A/C blow across his exposed backside. His hankering to use the facilities warred with an ingrained manly pride that said it was wrong to show off his naked butt. He certainly didn't pretend to be holier than the Pope, but neither was he in the habit of displaying his man parts to a woman he didn't know.

"Is this enough for today?" Binney queried quietly. "I'll help you back into bed and you can try again tomorrow."

"No," he grated. "When I get to the bathroom you don't have to stay with me, do you?"

"I do until you can navigate better on your own and not require help getting up off the commode, Rio. Earlier you mentioned at least one older injury. Did all modesty not go out the window then?"

"Even when I had the concussion I walked on my own. So, no, I handled everything I needed to do in privacy." Sucking in a deep breath, he took a tentative step forward.

"I'm glad to hear that solid breath," Dr. Layton said from behind Rio. "That tells me your lungs are performing well. Tomorrow, Dr. Darnell, the orthopedic doctor I've asked to see you, wants an MRI on your neck. He'll decide if you need cervical vertebrae four and five fused or not."

Rio straightened swiftly, a movement that caused

him to swear. "Uh, sorry. I don't like the sounds of fusion. Will that mean I can't turn my head?" His question came out in fits and spurts, because Binney gripped him tighter and they were inching toward the open bathroom door.

"That's something you'll have to ask Dr. Darnell." Layton spoke over the sound of his pager going off. "Blast it all, I'm on call and ER is sending an auto accident victim to surgery. Binney, you seem to be holding up okay. Would you rather I help get Rio back to bed? I've already written orders to get him up in the morning."

"It's up to Rio. I'm good so far."

Rio was close to choosing to return to bed rather than be left alone with Binney for such an intimate excursion, when Janet Valenzuela rushed back into the room.

"Land sakes! That looks painfully slow. Here, let me get on his other side. Ditch that crutch for now. I'll support you so you can hop a little faster."

"I'll leave you in their capable hands," Layton said, striding toward the door. "I will check you again on morning rounds. It'll be after I consult with Dr. Darnell."

Watching the surgeon dash out, Rio had no idea why he'd feel relieved to have a totally strange woman witnessing his humiliation. Possibly it had something to do with Janet being more the age of his mother. In fact he knew she had sons in their twenties. Maybe he could find a way to dismiss Binney without sounding ungrateful. Especially if, as it appeared, he was going to need to hire her for a while in order to leave the hospital. His fervent hope was that by then he could work the crutches enough on his own to not need help getting to the bathroom.

Between them, the nurses maneuvered their patient into the small bathroom. It so happened that Janet entered first. With her short but plump body and Rio's six-foot-two-inch rangy frame filling the space, Binney was left unable to fit inside.

She disengaged her hold on Rio's waist and slid her hand the length of his right arm so he could maintain balance as the older nurse helped him be seated.

"Here, I'll close the pocket door to give you some privacy," Binney murmured, backing fully out. "Holler when you're ready for a return trek to bed. By the way, Janet, we noticed his gown needs tying farther down the back." Her words were cut off as she shut the pair into the small space.

Rather than hover outside, Binney hurried back to straighten the rumpled bedsheets and fluff up Rio's pillow. She'd unhinged the right bedrail to get him up. Now she checked the left one to make sure it was secured. The last thing he'd need would be to fall out of bed in the middle of the night. As it was she couldn't help but think how tall and broad-shouldered he'd grown since she'd last seen him that evening in his cap and gown. She had thought about the McNabb twins over the ensuing years. Texas was big on rodeos and their accomplishments were often in the Abilene news. Rio and Ryder were home-grown boys who made names for themselves on the professional rodeo circuit. She assumed their rodeo accomplishments were a big part of who they were.

She gave the pillow a last thump, feeling sympathy for Rio, who in all likelihood was going to lose a career that had helped make him more popular. However, he'd been brought up having the fallback of a ranch, and he hadn't sounded disgruntled.

As she responded to Janet's call that they were ready for her again, Binney made a mental note to take a run out to said ranch tomorrow. What had Rio called it? Lonesome Road. The name didn't denote a place rolling out a welcome mat.

"Thanks for your help," Janet told Binney after they returned Rio to his bed.

"Yes, thank you," he rushed to add. "Listen, the doctors gave me your business card, Binney. Now that I know I can navigate to and from the bathroom with a little support, I'll probably check out of here next week. Depending on how I'm doing, if I need your services I'll give you a jingle. Okay?"

The two nurses exchanged slight frowns. It was Janet who said, "The doctors may move you from ICU to a room next week. But did Dr. Layton or Dr. Mason not tell you that you won't qualify for release home until you can get around with crutches all on your own?"

"They did. But we'll see. I'll recover faster at home," he ended with a plainly dismissive note.

"A lot will depend on whether or not you need those vertebrae fused, Rio," Binney reminded him.

He closed his eyes and didn't respond.

Binney sighed. "Right! Okay, bye, guys. It's late."
Shrugging, Binney left. She'd been here two hours
past her ER shift. She had noticed they'd scheduled
her the next day for the 11:00 p.m. to 3:00 a.m. slot
again. While she appreciated having the ability to
earn money between private duty nursing jobs, she
sometimes wondered if it'd be better to go back to
hospital duty altogether, where her hours would be
more consistent.

THINKING HIMSELF ALONE again at last, Rio yawned.
He opened his eyelids a crack when he felt fingers
wrap around his right wrist.

It was Janet taking his pulse. "I can see you're
wiped out from the exertion of hobbling to the bathroom. I want to be sure we didn't put a strain on your
heart or lungs." Dropping his wrist, she donned her
stethoscope and had him breathe in and out normally.

"All sounds good." She patted his hand and engaged the bed's side rail. "Murph told me you hate
the pain shots, but I have to give one. Doctor's orders. He also wants you to eat some yogurt." She
brought a carton over and removed the lid. Arrang-
ing double pillows behind him, she handed him the
container and a plastic spoon.

"I'd rather have a hamburger." After saying this,
Rio dug into the yogurt and ate it all in about four
spoonfuls.

"You'll be on soft foods awhile. At least until after
they see if you need vertebrae surgery." She whisked

away the empty carton. "Okay, Rio. Sorry, but it's shot time."

"Tired as I am right now, just give it to me. I hope I'll feel a whole lot better after a full night's sleep."

The nurse disposed of the container, logged on and wrote on his chart then went to a tray an aide had brought in. She picked up a preloaded syringe and checked that it was the right medication.

"Before you hit me with that, can you tell me a little bit about Binney?"

Janet eyed him quizzically. "What do you want to know? She's an A-1 nurse. Everyone who has ever worked with her says so. Far as I know there's not a person on staff who she doesn't get along with. And she does more than what's required. If you're wanting gossip, I've never heard any." She rubbed an alcohol wipe over his upper arm.

"She claims we went to the same high school. It bugs me that I can't remember her."

"I can't help you there. About the time you two were in high school I was through nursing school and was probably long married. This will sting," she warned, jabbing the short needle through his skin. "If you want my advice, you'd be smarter to hire Binney rather than spend a couple of weeks out at the rehab. There you'll be one sheep in a flock, if you get my meaning. At home with one-on-one care—well, think about it, you'll be the recipient of all the attention."

Rio closed his eyes. He had been thinking about

all that individual attention from the pretty nurse with the smooth hands and sparkling green eyes.

AFTER FINALLY LEAVING the hospital around 2:00 a.m. Binney only managed to sleep until ten o'clock in the morning. There were no calls or text messages on her cell phone. But had she really thought Rio McNabb would get in touch so soon asking to hire her?

Maybe she didn't want to work for him, she thought in the middle of scrambling eggs for breakfast. The hospital would keep her busy until some other private duty job came up.

At the very least, supposing he did offer her a position, she ought to inspect his ranch first and judge for herself if it was more isolated than she cared to be cooped up on with a young, too-handsome cowboy.

Thank heavens for GPS, she thought an hour later when finally she turned her motorcycle onto a graveled ranch road that led to the Lonesome Road horse ranch. Binney wondered how her predecessor ever found her way around this rural community without one.

She slowed considerably as a flock of wild turkeys flapped across the road in front of her. The road wound through high desert brush, shaded along the way by gorgeous old live oak trees. A moment before the road opened up to a clearing, Binney spotted a white-tailed deer bounding through a thicket of mesquite and juniper.

As she stopped completely to take the measure of a stone ranch house that had a wide porch running clear across the front of the structure, a fuzzy-faced barking dog ran up to her. She bent to let him sniff her hand and then gave him a rub when he rolled over. She supposed someone was on the property caring for the animal. From reading his chart Binney knew Rio McNabb wasn't married. But she hadn't thought ahead to wonder if he had a live-in. A lot of cowboys did. And surely a man as handsome as Rio could have his pick of any number of rodeo followers. She refused to refer to them as buckle bunnies because that was so demeaning.

Continuing to pet the friendly dog, she eyed a windmill that told her the ranch was on a well. Two barns in the distance boasted new paint, as did split-rail fences that enclosed grassy pens where several beautiful golden horses grazed in late summer sunlight.

As she rose from where she had crouched to pet the dog, thinking to stroll over for a closer look at the horses, a man seated atop a long-legged horse appeared out of nowhere, bearing down on her.

He pulled the snorting horse to a standstill even as Binney scrambled out of its path. The dog barked louder, and ran circles around the dancing horse.

"Are you lost?" the rider asked. He removed his hat and she met the dark, curious gaze of a handsome man, probably a few years older than Rio.

"No. I came in search of the Lonesome Road Ranch. I'm Binney Taylor, the area's visiting nurse. It's not definite the ranch owner will request my nursing services when he's released from the hospital. But since his surgeon recommended me and Mr. McNabb and I spoke about the possibility, I came out to get the lay of the land. I apologize if I interrupted your work."

The man swung out of the saddle. "I'm JJ Montoya. I train horses for Rio, and look after the ranch whenever he's away. I only spoke briefly to him yesterday. He was more concerned about the horse that injured him than he was about much else except making sure I collected his pickup, camper and Tagalong, here," he added, indicating the dog that had gone to lie across Binney's feet. "Tag doesn't generally trust strangers. He seems to like you."

Bending, Binney scratched the animal behind his floppy ears. "I'd love to have a dog or cat, but since my work out in the community often takes me away from my apartment for weeks at a time, I can't have one."

"How is Rio, really?" the man still holding the reins of the golden horse asked suddenly. "He didn't sound his old self. But from the list of all he said was wrong with him, I frankly doubted he'd be home very soon."

Dusting off her hands, Binney hiked a shoulder. "Sorry, I can't discuss a patient's condition. I do know he had more evaluations scheduled for this morning. You could phone him later and get an update. Uh, it's nice to meet you, Mr. Montoya, but I won't keep you. You may or may not see me again, depending on whether or not I become part of Mr.

McNabb's recovery team. However, let me say this is a beautiful ranch."

Pausing, Binney let her gaze roam over the scenic valley. She pictured what it might have been like growing up here, and felt a twinge of regret she always felt when forced to remember how she'd never had a real home or family.

Waving goodbye, she called, "It definitely wouldn't be a hardship to take an assignment here." She left the property with a greater appreciation for Rio's ranch than when she'd first turned off the main highway onto the lonely road.

RIO FINISHED HIS lunch of cream of tomato soup and custard, wishing again for something more substantial. But he was being promised more for supper. The orthopedic doctor had come to see him after the MRI. He said he thought the cracked vertebrae would heal by themselves if Rio minded his p's and q's and didn't do anything to reinjure his neck. In fact, Darnell wrote an order to move him out of ICU into a two-bed ward later that afternoon. He planned to recheck Rio at the end of the following week, and said if nothing changed he'd discharge him, providing he use something called a TENS Unit, designed to promote faster bone repair. Darnell also said he'd have a tech order up a better-fitting neck collar.

All in all Rio was feeling pretty good. Especially since he'd also asked about cutting back the pain medication, and Dr. Darnell said they'd try less potent pills instead of shots.

His cell phone rang. Picking it up off his tray where the nurse had set it, Rio saw the call was from JJ.

"Hi, buddy. How goes everything at the ranch?"

"Funny, I'm calling to ask how it goes at the hospital."

"Some better." Rio launched into telling his ranch hand all he'd learned.

"So, you think you'll get to come home next weekend? Then you've settled on hiring yourself a home nurse?"

"I haven't decided. Why?"

"Well, now," JJ drawled, "Binney Taylor came out to take a gander at the ranch. She's some looker, boss. Tag liked her so much if she'd been a burglar he'd have invited her in and showed her the silverware."

"Binney drove out to the ranch?"

"Drove isn't the right term. Not only is the lady damned pretty, but she rides a Harley like a pro."

"She what?"

"You got hearing problems? The gal showed up here astraddle of a big old hog. She won over your dog, who usually bares his teeth at strangers. Oh, and before she left she said you have a nice ranch and it wouldn't be a hardship to work here."

Someone came into his room and removed his lunch tray, but Rio didn't acknowledge her. His brain had stalled out picturing the tall slender nurse with soft, soft hands and gorgeous eyes, riding a motorcycle. He then imagined her legs clamped around one of his horses. That image quickly morphed into one where, whole again, he reclined in his king bed, and those same long, luscious legs straddled his hips with just the right amount of pressure.

"Rio, you still there?" JJ whistled into the phone.

Barely managing to say "Yeah" in gruff tones, Rio reined in derelict visions he chalked up to pain and forced inactivity. "Listen, I'm gonna have to call you back later, JJ." He hit disconnect and willed away the all-too-enjoyable snapshot lodged in his head.

Chapter Three

Dr. Layton stopped by Rio's hospital room and told him he'd turned over his care to the orthopedist. "My job as your surgeon is finished. Your lung remains inflated. All else are bone injuries that are Dr. Darnell's field of expertise. I hear he's moving you from ICU. He'll be the one you'll be fighting with about going into rehab."

Rio screwed his lips to one side then said, "Since I'd rather recover at home I'm going to hire Nurse Taylor. Do you have any idea how long I may need her help? Or is that something I should ask Dr. Darnell?"

"Just judging from your initial injuries, I'd say you'll need a month to six weeks to get you moving under your own power. Darnell can pinpoint that better after he sees follow-up X-rays of your broken wrist and clavicle."

Layton turned to the computer and pulled up Rio's chart. "I see he ordered a TENS Unit to help heal the vertebrae. That requires removing the cervical collar to sit with the electronic device on your neck for a specified time each day. Getting the collar off and on properly will take assistance. Frankly, I still don't get what you have against going to rehab. They're staffed for maximum therapies."

Rio puffed out a disgusted sigh. "I like being in control of my life. Isn't that true of everyone?"

"Yes, unless you're sick or injured. I notice you listed your parents as next of kin. Can they help you at home?"

"If they weren't on their dream trip to Australia they would be my go-to people. Worrier that my mom is, I hope they don't hear of my accident. They'd cut their trip short. You may think I'm unreasonable. As a rule I'm not."

"I see a lot of you cowboy types. Don't blame me for thinking you all have more guts than sense. I do wish you luck." The doctor closed out the computer, shook hands with Rio and then left the room.

Rio barely had time to gather his thoughts when the team scheduled to move him to a ward arrived. Two burly guys dressed in green scrubs transferred him, mattress and all, onto a gurney, while an aide gathered his personal belongings. She'd headed out when Rio called to her. "Did you pick up a business card for a private duty nurse?"

"I left it in the drawer. I heard Gertrude Murphy and Janet Valenzuela talking. I thought they said you weren't going to hire…uh, never mind. I'll grab the card." She turned back and slipped past the gurney.

Rio would have liked to know what he'd said to give the ICU nurses the impression he wasn't going to hire Binney. If word got back to her, she might take another job. He thought he'd been clear to everyone about wanting to recuperate at home, but weigh his options. As soon as he got settled in a ward he'd phone her and ask about her fees.

He did just that as soon as the transfer team left.

Binney sounded surprised to hear from him. "I charge the going daily rate for in-home nursing care unless I do household chores. There's a greater daily charge if I do cooking, laundry or other housework." She named both amounts.

"Which one includes taking care of a pet? I know you went out to my ranch and met my dog. JJ said you and Tag hit it off. I'm sure he was mistreated before I found him. He's not usually trusting of strangers, so you're an exception."

"I hate hearing he may have been mistreated. Goodness, he seemed such a loving dog. Care for him would be included in either rate." She paused then added, "Mr. Montoya was nice. What I viewed of your ranch was lovely. I hope you aren't annoyed that I went to check it over. It's something I do if the opportunity presents itself before I decide to take a job."

"Has a preview caused you to turn any job down?"

"Once. The old guy raised goats and lived in a one-room shack back in the hills. He had pneumonia and needed care, but a requirement of mine is to have my own bedroom. I never asked the size of your home. Wait…didn't you indicate it's where you grew up, so it'd be a family home layout, right?"

"It is. You'd have a bedroom. I bought the ranch from my folks. They wanted to retire to San Antonio. At the moment they're on a trip out of the country. What about you? Does your family still live in Abilene?"

"I live there. I rent an efficiency apartment downtown. Tell you what, Rio. My contract spells everything out. I work a late-late shift in ER tonight. It'll be past visiting hours when I get to the hospital. But I'll leave a copy at the unit desk and tomorrow you can ask a nurse to bring it in for you to read over. I want you to be satisfied."

"We both need to be satisfied." Rio couldn't help flashing back to his earlier thoughts of the two of them in his big bed. Shoot, not only wasn't he in any shape for monkey business, keeping hands off was probably listed in her contract. "So you know, I'd require some cooking and other stuff. I hope if Dr. Darnell sees I have home care, he'll release me quicker."

"Murph told me two things you balked at were renting a hospital bed and going home by ambulance. Both are most apt to impress Dr. Darnell."

Rio grunted, then said, "I'll see. So, we'll touch base soon?"

"Roger that."

Noting that she'd disconnected, Rio set his phone on the tray table. He tried to find a comfortable position as he closed his eyes and pictured all five foot eight inches of Nurse Taylor.

He woke up, not knowing how much time had

passed, to a high-pitched feminine voice exclaim-
ing, "Eew, Sugar Bear! You look awful. How do
you feel?"

He smelled Traci Walker's signature perfume before she came close enough to identify. He failed to
escape before she bent and brushed a damp kiss on
his lips. "Just what I want to hear, how bad I look,
Traci. As to how I feel, I've been better."

She straightened away. "Daddy and Mama told
me about your accident. I just got home last night
from visiting Samantha in the Big Apple. We saw
Ryder ride in Madison Square Garden." She pouted,
a sulky face Rio knew she'd long perfected as they'd
grown up together and had even dated a few times.

She continued discussing her trip. "We tried talking Ryder into hitting a few nightclubs with us. He's
so focused on amassing points, he told Sammi he had
to ride the next morning. You know she used to always wrap him around her finger. Ryder's changed.
But we snagged Ben Jarvis and still danced the night
away." Traci spun away from the bed and peered
around, wrinkling her nose. "So when can you leave
this horrid, smelly place?"

Rio managed a brief inspection of her expression
of distaste. She hadn't changed since she'd unexpect-
edly popped in to see him at the Fort Worth rodeo
in the spring and tried to steamroll him into renew-
ing their long-dead relationship. Her daddy, Weldon
Walker, owned the biggest ranch around Abilene. He
was a leading patron of the PRCA. Traci, a six-time
rodeo queen, dabbled in charity work with her mom.

It surprised Rio to hear that his brother had skipped going out with her sister, a New York model. In high school Ryder had dated Samantha longer than he'd stuck with any girl.

"Before I check out I need to hire nursing care and the services of a chief cook and bottle washer at the ranch," Rio said. "Any chance you're in the mood to volunteer?" he asked in jest, knowing her family had always employed a cook themselves.

True to his expectations, she rolled her eyes. "I might lend a hand if you didn't live in the sticks. You need to sell and buy a ranch closer to town. You and I could be good together if you didn't bury yourself miles from civilization. I need to be near town, because Daddy's buying me a boutique."

"What do you mean, we could be good together?"

She wiggled her ring finger. "Daddy says it's time you pop the question and we get married, Sugar Bear."

"What?" Rio knew he was guilty of gaping.

"You're so stubborn, but I can wear you down."

"Don't count on it. You're a partier and I like solitude. And I'll never sell the Lonesome Road. Raising horses out there is all I've ever wanted to do."

"How can you say that when you've been on the rodeo circuit for years? Daddy said Abilene might be your last rodeo, though. I predict you'll get bored soon enough. Oh, but starting tomorrow I'm helping Mama arrange the country club's harvest ball. Heavens, Sugar Bear, can you even get out of bed? From my observation you'll need more help than anyone

I know can give. Maybe Lola Vickers. Shall I have
Mama call her?"

"Lola's retired." Suddenly recalling how tight the
area ranch teens used to be, he blurted, "Do you remember Binney Taylor from high school?"

Traci assumed an annoyed expression. "Why ever
would you ask about her? Surely you know she got
her name because she was left on the doorstep at
the orphanage in one of those green vegetable trash
bins. Iona Taylor found her. She assigned the little
nobody her last name. Mama said Binney lived in
different foster homes, but she never fit in and never
got along. By high school they sent her to a group
home run by Catholic nuns."

Traci's diatribe left a sour taste in Rio's mouth.
"Well, she's a registered nurse now. Sometimes she
works here, but also does private nursing jobs. I plan
to hire her."

Traci swiveled her head around as if searching for
the woman they were discussing. "Land sakes. You
can't get mixed up with the likes of her. Mama would
bar you from the country club. And what would your
folks say? Binney Taylor's not like us. Why, nobody
knows her roots."

Disliking the turn of this conversation, Rio
couldn't have been happier when a ward nurse came
in, interrupting Traci's rant about Binney.

"Visiting hours are over," the nurse announced.
"It's time for Mr. McNabb's meds. You'll have to
come back later this evening, or tomorrow."

At first Rio thought Traci would throw her

wealthy weight around and refuse to go. As it was she merely tightened her grip on her designer purse and said, "I only had a few minutes to spare on my way to a mani-pedi appointment anyway. I'll call you, Sugar Bear. If you're up and around in time for the Harvest Ball the first of October, I'll arrange a ticket. I'll even drive out to the boonies and pick you up."

Rio laughed. "Have you really looked closely at me, Traci? I won't be doin' any boot scootin' boogying by October. Oh, tell your dad I'm glad his horse is okay even if Diablo Colorado did his best to kill us both in the arena."

She paused at the door. "Don't you forget how important Daddy is in the rodeo/ranching community. He could help you build your horse trade if you don't do something foolish like let a person in your home that Lord only knows her background." She blew Rio a kiss and swept from the room on her red spiked heels.

The nurse stared for a moment at the empty doorway then set a small cup of pills on Rio's tray table. She poured him a glass of water from an icy pitcher. "Our ward has strict rules for visitation. We sometimes make allowances for relatives," she said pointedly, again eyeing the door.

"She's not a relative." It was all Rio could do to hide a smile when the nurse appeared relieved. "What are these for?" he asked when the woman, whose name tag read Suzette Ferris RN, dumped three pills into his hand.

"One is an antibiotic. I'm about to unhook your

IV. The other two are painkillers. Dr. Darnell re-
placed the shots you were receiving. If these keep
your pain at bay, he'll likely order them for a couple of weeks. Be sure to tell us if they aren't strong
enough. I heard you'd rather be off everything, but
truthfully, hurting isn't good."

"Are they addictive?"

"They could be if you were on them for an extended period of time. Our physicians are careful
about that."

Popping all three pills in his mouth, Rio swallowed them down with one gulp from the glass. He
took the spoon and container of custard she'd opened.
"How long before I can have real food?"

"If by real food you mean steak, probably not until
it's easier for you to get up and around."

"Not necessarily steak, but even a sandwich. If all
I get is baby food, won't that delay how soon I have
the strength to get up and around?"

There was a rustling at the door and Rio raised
his head, fearing Traci had returned. But Binney
Taylor walked in. She wore jeans, boots and a plaid
blouse. Her small waist was circled by a two-inch-
wide leather belt. Her smile stretched from ear to
ear. For the first time Rio noticed a smattering of
appealing freckles on her creamy cheeks. He found
it difficult to swallow.

"Is he giving you a hard time, Suzette? Knock
it off, McNabb. She's one of the best darned nurses
on this ward."

Nurse Ferris rushed to hug Binney. "Look who's

talking. If you're a friend of this guy, you're far superior to his last visitor," she said, lowering her voice.

Appearing a tad confused, Binney waved an envelope. "I'm bringing Rio one of my private duty contracts to go over. I intended to drop it at the ward desk since I'm working the late shift in ER. But I got a call from Mabel in administration. She said if I'm slated to accompany Rio home, Dr. Darnell may release him soon. He needs time to decide between my services or going to Baxter Rehab."

Suzette wrinkled her nose. "No contest to my way of thinking. Especially as he's bugging me for *real* food." She made quote marks in the air when she said real. Facing Rio, she added, "When Binney worked here full-time she often brought casseroles to our lunch room. All of the nurses fought to see who'd get there first."

Her pager went off. Excusing herself, she air-kissed Binney and dashed from the room.

Binney covered the distance to the bed, set the envelope on Rio's tray table and relieved him of the empty custard container he still held. She stepped on the lever to open the waste container, then stopped. "Are they monitoring what you eat and excrete?"

"What? I'm not getting enough food to excrete anything," he said, turning red.

"They'll give you something more substantial tomorrow. You have to prove your intestines work well before you can go home, you know."

His eyebrows dived together. "I actually don't know. I was only in a hospital ER last time I was

thrown from a horse." He tried casting his eyes elsewhere, but he was hampered by the cervical collar.

"I told you modesty flies out the window when
you're dealing with extensive injuries. If you turn
red as a tomato whenever it's time to shower, get a
lotion rubdown or at other pertinent times, it's pointless for us to try to work together."

He studied her for a long moment. "It'll be hard
for me to put aside long-held proprieties, but I want
to hire you." He hurriedly added, "I'll sign the contract now."

"But you haven't read it," Binney said.

"With all the recommendations you've had from
staff here, I shouldn't have waited this long. Do you
have a pen?" He didn't say there was someone who
hadn't recommended her. But Traci Walker's com-
ments were one reason he wanted to sign on the dotted line and show folks like Traci and her family that
not every area rancher gave a damn about their view
of someone's roots.

Binney took the papers out of the envelope. "I'll
run out to the nursing station and grab a pen while
you go over this. Have you compared home care to
what all is offered at Baxter Rehab?"

"I'm not going there. Call it plain pigheadedness.
Initially I held out hope I could handle healing at
home on my own. I'm stubborn, but not stupid. I'll
need help."

"In that respect you aren't a lone wolf, Rio. Just
since I took over private duty nursing from Lola, vir-
tually every rancher who hired me has shared your

feelings about being tended to by a strange woman. Some called me a wet-behind-the-ears kid. At first I resented it. Now I understand. There's a loss of dignity attached to needing help with the basics of one's life. Keep in mind it's temporary."

"I hope so," he said, sounding so unsure Binney hesitated at the door and peered back over her shoulder.

"Did Dr. Darnell downgrade your prognosis? I thought Janet said he's fairly sure you won't require fusion of the vertebrae."

Rio tried to shrug, but was assailed by a pain so sharp in his back that it took his breath away.

Binney rushed back to his side. "What is it, Rio? Not your lung again?"

"No." He ground his back teeth and took a slow breath. "Higher and in my back." He raised his right hand up to his left shoulder and discovered the cast wouldn't allow him to rub where it hurt. "Dammit," he growled, dropping his arm to his side again. Closing his eyes, he took a deep breath as Binney ran her cool fingers under the neck of his dressing gown.

"Sorry I swore. Bad habit," he admitted. "Wow! That feels better, whatever you did."

"I'm guessing the brace for your fractured clavicle is twisted. Maybe in transferring you from ICU. While I'm at the desk picking up a pen I'll ask one of the orthopedic nurses to see if Dr. Darnell will order a fresh one." She lightly massaged the skin under the scrunched material.

"Man, that's nice. If I was a cat I'd purr."

"I'm happy to hear it didn't restrict your sense of humor." Smiling, she said, "Hang in there. I'll be right back."

It was Suzette and another nurse Rio hadn't seen before who next entered his room.

"Why didn't you tell me we needed to check your clavicle brace," Suzette scolded, motioning for the second woman to help her sit Rio up with his feet dangling over the side of his bed. "Dr. Darnell left standing orders to change your cervical collar and clavicle brace anytime you got uncomfortable."

They'd shut the door, but he still felt exposed when Suzette untied his dressing gown and let it fall to pool around his waist. The newcomer steadied him while Nurse Ferris *tsked* and began to unfasten straps passing behind his back. "Removing the sling completely will cause pain," she warned. "Can you hold your breath until I can slip you into a fresh brace? By the way, this is Lacy. She's a fourth-year student nurse training here."

A sharp stitch stabbed Rio's back. "Where's Binney?" he asked, barely able to move his lips.

Suzette spoke from behind him. "She went downstairs to find a brochure on Baxter Rehab for you."

"Why? I said I want to sign her contract." He jerked his head up and unconsciously squared his shoulders. The pain nearly stole his ability to huff out, "Does she not want the job with me?"

Finally Suzette answered. "That's our Binney. She wants a patient to understand all choices." Dropping the old sling, she let her coworker steady Rio while she unfurled a new one.

BINNEY SPED SILENTLY into Rio's room and immediately pulled up short as her gaze honed in on the broad, muscled, bronzed chest of the man being propped up in bed. She nearly choked trying to take a breath, and her mouth went dry of its own volition.

In spite of wearing a cervical collar and having a wrist and ankle all casted or taped up, he represented a fabulous specimen of manhood. Wide chest tapering to slender hips, but with corded muscle in all the right places. Why had she ever thought his twin was more alluring?

But, she shouldn't be smitten by Rio, either. There were definite rules in a nurse-patient relationship. It was probably the main reason she pushed him to consider going to Baxter Rehab. Boy, howdy, she hadn't made allowance for possibly ministering to someone so near her age. Someone she'd once had on a pedestal along with his twin, until Ryder fell off.

She forced herself to quit gawking, but because she remained flustered, she dropped the pen and the brochure she'd gone after fluttered from her hand. The noise attracted the attention of the two nurses working behind Rio. And he attempted to check out the commotion.

"Oh, you're back," Suzette exclaimed. "I shouldn't ask, but can you give us a hand? Lacy's never done this before. In surgery they put him in this sling, but didn't add a strap at the back to hold his arm steady. Dr. Darnell won't want his arm flapping and causing him pain." She explained all of that for the sake of the student.

Binney rescued the pen and brochure, set them on Rio's tray table, and hurried over to the sink to wash before pitching in.

The two professionals made short work of getting Rio into the harness, but Binney's fingers had felt unsteady from unusual nervousness.

"Puts me in mind of bridling a horse," Rio grumbled. "Although, it sure feels better. Uh, but can you guide my arms into the gown thing?" He scowled. "How long do I have to wear it? Can I wear regular clothes at home? Even to go home," he stressed. "I'd hate for any rodeo fans to see me going out of here in what amounts to a dress."

Suzette winked at Binney. "And people call women vain." She assisted Rio into the sleeves of the striped gown, tied it securely and Lacy eased him back against the elevated head of his bed.

Binney took pity on Rio. "With your hand and wrist in a cast, you'll need loose-fitting, short-sleeved shirts. Until the doctor says you can quit taping the sprained ankle, I recommend two sizes too large pajamas, and later ripping a pair of jeans up several inches from the bottom. That way you'll look your old self for visitors."

"Thanks for easing my mind on that score. I knew a guy who went to Baxter after he got stomped on steer wrestling. They didn't let him wear jeans until he'd totally recovered. Just hand me the pen and your contract."

Suzette smiled, but because she still stood by his bed, she moved the tray table closer and slid him the items Binney had brought. "Here you go, tough guy. If wearing your own clothes is the criteria for hiring Binney instead of going to rehab, your decision seems made." She gathered up the discarded brace and restored both bed rails. "You know to press this button if you need us," she said, pointing to an area inside the rail.

"Got it." Lifting his eyes, he asked, "Why two copies of the same thing?"

"One is yours, and I get one," she said. "Like any contract. Did you read it?"

"I'm too tired after all the fuss changing my brace. I want to go home, and you're the best, if not the only, game in town." Rio scribbled his name on the second set of papers and dropped the pen. He shut his eyes. "If someone has time they can put my copy with my personal belongings. I'll find out what day I can leave when Dr. Darnell makes his rounds. I'll call you, Binney. Er…do I need to call you Nurse Taylor now?"

"No." Binney accepted her copy of the contract and watched Suzette store Rio's in a zippered bag with his boots and clothing he wore from the rodeo. "Home care is more relaxed about some things. However, with your extensive injuries, you will need that hospital bed we discussed. Plus, I know you argued against going home in an ambulance. But I've made one trip down the graveled road to your ranch, so book the ambulance, Rio."

Suzette seconded Binney's edict. "You don't want to jar any bones out of place rattling around in a pickup truck. I assume that was your original plan."

"It was. Okay… I'll call about an ambulance. But my ranch hand and I both own king-cab pickups." Opening one eye, Rio pinned Binney. "I imagine my ranch road would be jarring to someone riding a Harley. I hope you can drive a pickup in case JJ's tied up and you need to go for groceries or dog food."

"Of course," Binney said.

Suzette and Lacy gaped at her and gasped. "Really, you travel by motorcycle?" The older nurse whooped. "I'm impressed."

"Me, too," Lacy said as the three women headed out.

"I bought it when gas got so expensive," Binney acknowledged. "I like it, and I can pack everything I need medical-wise and my clothing in the saddle-bags."

They exited the room and the door swished closed behind them.

In the hall the student nurse dashed off to join a floor nurse who'd beckoned her. Suzette leaned over and confessed to Binney, "I envy you getting to work outside the hospital setting."

"Private duty is great if the people you work for are pleasant. Some can be overly cantankerous and if you're the only nurse there's no respite."

"Rio McNabb hasn't caused us any angst so far.

Of course I can't say the same if you have to deal very often with his rich-bitch girlfriend."

Grinding to a halt, Binney's jaw dropped. "Who? I didn't know he had a girlfriend." She bit her lip. "Actually no one's ever said he didn't. Do you know her?"

"No, thank heavens. I know her type. Everything she had on screamed money. And she skirted me like I was dirt. You'd know how rich she is, too, because she talked to Rio about picking him up for the country club's October ball. I've heard those tickets are five thousand dollars each."

Binney nodded. "A youth center I do some counseling at was their charity one year. I think most of their funds go to local good causes." For some reason her stomach still pitched at the thought of Rio having a girlfriend of privilege. But why wouldn't he? His family had owned a big ranch, and now he did.

"You're so bighearted. I'm not as magnanimous when it comes to rich snobs."

"Having wealth does go to some people's heads." Binney thought back to her school days, when certain girls had been especially cutting and mean. "I hope Rio isn't seriously involved with a woman like that. I can believe that, though, of his twin," she mused. "Oh, maybe you aren't aware that I knew them growing up. Rich girls, poor girls, all girls in school were enamored of both. Ryder dated a super-rich girl, I know. Maybe Rio's trying to outshine his brother." She winked as she said it, and Suzette laughed.

"I've gotta run. If I don't see you again until after

you wind down your tenure at McNabb's," the ward nurse whispered, making sure no one else heard, "let's get together for lunch. Should you meet Ms. Rich Witch, I'll be anxious to hear if you concur with my assessment."

"Sure. I may go by St. Gertrude's and light a couple of candles to hopefully ward off the possibility." Binney took her leave, dwelling on what a seemingly down-to-earth cowboy like Rio might see in a woman of the type Suzette had described.

When it came down to it, why did she care what type woman either McNabb twin dated? It was past time she killed and buried a decade-old crush that had ended badly for her. Although she'd be first to admit the way Ryder had treated her had long-affected her willingness to trust men.

Chapter Four

Three days later, Binney hadn't heard from Rio and so was considering a different private duty job in Sweetwater, which was farther afield than she normally traveled, when the call from Rio came. Even though she'd more than half hoped to hear from him, when she saw his name on her cell phone she had to take a deep breath before answering, and hoped she sounded normal. "Hi, Rio. Sorry I haven't been up to the ward to see you again. I've worked double shifts in ER. Truthfully, I'd about decided you'd changed your mind and decided to go to Baxter Rehab after all."

"Gosh, no. Doc Darnell finally said I can go home tomorrow afternoon. It's short notice, but are you available to start working for me then? Please say yes. I'm going stir-crazy."

"I thought your release was imminent the other day. I hope you haven't developed additional problems."

"Not that I know of."

"Okay, so you're totally set?"

"Yep. Yesterday JJ rented a hospital bed. And he got one of those shower seat things Nurse Farris suggested. He said a medical supply place delivered that electronic gadget that Doc wants me to wear an hour or so every day."

"It's the TENS Unit."

"Right. And this morning Doc Darnell said I can leave anytime after one tomorrow. Once you say what time you can meet me at the ranch I'll book an ambulance and finally get home and breathe some fresh air."

Binney laughed. "You can't fool me. I know the aroma around a ranch is rarely fresh."

"Maybe it's an acquired preference," he drawled. "It's no worse than the antiseptic odors around here."

"Touché! It so happens the ER nurse I'm filling in for starts back tomorrow. So, if Discharge starts your paperwork right after lunch it'll probably be one thirty or so by the time they complete everything and transport you downstairs. How about if I plan to meet the ambulance at the entrance and follow you to the ranch?"

"Perfect. I'm so ready to blow this place and get back to normal."

"Rio, you do know you're trading all nursing done at the hospital for pretty much the same routine at your home? I mean, the kind of injuries you sustained take time to heal regardless of where you park your body."

"Yeah, I know. But Dr. Darnell said, depending on your evaluation, maybe in a week or so I can go out to see the horses. Is it dumb for me to think that'll be better for me than any medicine?"

"Not dumb, but it may prove discouraging for someone like you."

"Someone like me? What's that supposed to mean?" His tone vibrated with hurt.

"Nothing bad. Anyone can see you're a true cowboy, Rio. The genuine article. I doubt that in the past you've ever walked by anything at the ranch needing attention that you didn't stop and take care of it. Until all of your injured bones knit well, you simply can't do normal chores. Trying will set you back."

He was silent for so long, Binney thought maybe the call had dropped. "Rio?"

"I hear you. Can you just let me be excited about going home?"

Binney tightened her hold on her cell phone. She'd rained on his parade and he was pouting. Possibly it was a bad idea for her to take this assignment. Either he was more thin-skinned than she'd imagined, or she was more on edge thinking about riding herd on him.

"I didn't mean to snarl at you," he said. "Truce? I know I have to let you call the shots."

"I'm not an ogre, Rio. But I do take caring for my patients seriously."

"So I've heard. Believe it or not, it's why I want you for my home care."

"Okay. I accept your truce. We'll start our relationship tomorrow. Uh, our w-working relationship," she stuttered. Feeling heat climb her neck and cheeks, she disconnected the call without waiting for his response. Afterward she stood in the middle of her bedroom, holding the phone for a long time. *Why was she so darned nervous?* Having anticipated his call, she had packed medical supplies she figured to need for him. After previewing his remote ranch, she'd set out jeans and shirts. In essence she was ready to take the job. *But was her heart ready?*

Maybe a million times since he'd signed her contract she'd stared out her front window in the direction of his ranch and had given herself pep talks centered on spending weeks alone with him.

BINNEY USED HER last shift in ER to double down on professionalism. She did every assigned task by the book. When her shift ended, all of the ER docs told her how sorry they were to see her go. The chief of ER made a special point of saying he'd hire her back full-time in a heartbeat. His assertion provided her the grounding to face any challenge, including a too-handsome bronc rider who made her think of herself as a woman, not just a nurse.

Mulling that over, riding home on her bike she blamed her wonky feelings on how many of her impressionable years she'd given both of the McNabb twins a special spot in her lonely heart. While Rio had never paid her any attention, he'd never been cruel like a lot of other boys—like his brother. A lot of guys and girls had made fun of her hand-me-down clothes and the fact she lived in a group home, or they'd rudely joked about the fact no parent had ever wanted her. At first she'd gone to each foster home thinking it would be her forever family. All had disappointed her. She did still long for a family, but shift work and erratic hours stood in her way of making time to date. Really she had yet to meet anyone special enough to make her dream of marriage.

THE NEXT MORNING Binney finished her minimal packing then took items from her fridge that would spoil if left until her job ended. She lugged the box of perishable foods over to her elderly neighbor.

"Mildred, I'm glad you can use my leftover milk, eggs and cheese."

"I'm happy to get these things, girl. Grocery prices keep rising. For those of us on a fixed income it means we sometimes have to give up items like eggs and cheese. You say you'll be working out on another ranch? I miss the good old days my husband, may he rest in peace, and I raised cattle south out of Robert Lee. Hard to believe Bill's been gone thirty years." The woman shifted the sack of food and filtered a pale blue-veined hand through white locks. "I'll keep an eye on your apartment, Binney. Only place I go these days is to church. I know your job as a nurse is to take care of somebody sick, but try to grab some time to enjoy the wide open spaces. Even our medium-sized town keeps growing. With more people comes more pollution. There are times I wish my brother-in-law hadn't sold the ranch and moved me here."

"You're sounding a bit maudlin. Are you feeling

okay? I have an hour before I need to meet the ambulance that will be taking my patient to his ranch. Can I run to the store for you? You're not out of the vitamins your doctor wants you to take, are you?"

"Bless you, child. I still have half a bottle. I will sorely miss you popping by to sit a spell and talk. Or bringing your guitar to play tunes for me. I know that will cheer up your new patient, though."

"I hadn't set my guitar out to take. Did you see on TV a couple of weeks ago about the rodeo bronc rider who had a horse fall on him? That's who I'll be taking care of. Guys like that spend a lot of evenings on the road in cities where there are top Western bands and singers performing. I'm self-taught and only mess around for my own pleasure."

"And mine. You sound real good to me. I recognize all of the songs you play. Take it, Binney. If that poor cowboy is as stove-up as they said on TV, he'll be restless. I recollect hearing somebody say that music soothes the savage beast. My Bill always sang to our cattle to calm 'em down."

"You talked me into it." Binney gave the frail woman a gentle hug. "Take care and watch that you don't fall on our stairs. If you need something, call me. I'm staying in the country and won't be able to run over here, but I have a list of friends I know will help."

"The world needs more young folks like you. If that cowboy doesn't have a lady at home, and if he's blessed with half a brain, he'll charm you into sticking around his ranch. Not that I'm anxious to lose you as a neighbor. But a nice, pretty girl like you ought to be settled down with someone to love and be loved by."

Binney laughed, but knew she'd blushed. "Don't hold your breath, Mildred. A nurse on the hospital ward where he's currently being treated told me he has a girlfriend." From the way Suzette spoke, she crossed her fingers that the woman wouldn't drop by to see him at the ranch. But as big as his ranch was, she could make herself scarce. She could always take his dog for a walk, or go see the horses.

"My hope is you'll marry someone who appreciates you, Binney. I'm going to light a candle for you at church. So there."

Binney's smile was weaker. "You do that. Yikes, we've talked half my time away. I have to go. Bye, Mildred." She gave the woman another hug then darted across the hall into her apartment, where she collected everything she thought she'd need at the ranch, including hanging her guitar case across her back.

Fifteen minutes later she rolled into the turnaround in front of the hospital right behind the ambulance.

Binnie knew Jorge, the EMT who hopped out of the vehicle and came to the back to remove the gurney he and the driver would take inside to receive Rio.

Jorge saw her, because he handed off the gurney to the driver and walked back to speak to her. "Hi, Binney. Are you going out on this case?"

"I am. How's your family?"

He beamed. "Good. Real good. Thanks for asking. I have a week's vacation coming. My wife booked a hotel at Padre Island."

"Your kids will love it. It sounds wonderful. Mine are always working vacations." She chuckled.

"The ranch where you're going is out in the sticks. The hot, dry sticks."

"I visited it. It's pretty. There were trees, wildlife, and his ranch is situated at the foot of rolling hills. A nice change from the city."

"You always look on the bright side of things. Hey, I gotta go help Leo get our patient. Since you've been out there, how about if we follow you?"

"Sure, but will you tell the patient I'll be leading the way so he knows I'm here? Most of the ranch road is dirt or gravel. By leading I won't be eating your dust."

The man signified he'd heard by giving a two-fingered salute before jogging off. Binney kick-started her Harley, donned her helmet and pulled to the front of the ambulance, where she waited until they emerged with the rolling bed.

This time it didn't seem so far out to the Lonesome Road. Binney figured that was because she didn't have to keep consulting her GPS on her cell phone. The hot September sun had shifted in the sky into the western sector enough to send its blistering rays over the stone house and outlying barn and sheds by the time they arrived.

After removing her helmet, Binney hung it on

the back and shook out her sweat-damp hair. As she squinted at the shimmering sun, she was thankful she'd managed to get her natural curls cut shorter for however long she'd be out here.

Even though she could feel the sweat beneath the leather guitar case lashed across her back, she didn't unbuckle it when she wheeled her bike over to park it in a slim section of shade.

Leo had turned the ambulance around and backed as close to the three steps leading up to the wide porch as possible. Binney joined him, introduced herself, and they walked to the back of the vehicle where Jorge had already flung open the door.

She'd barely greeted Rio when out of nowhere came a snarling, barking dog that leaped at Leo and nipped his arm.

First to recover from the shock, Binney grabbed the animal's collar. "Tag, Tag," she said softly, but firmly. "We're friends who have brought your master home."

Seeming to recognize her, the big fuzzy Labradoodle released the stranger's shirt sleeve and nuzzled his head against Binney's thigh. That only lasted until Jorge called to Leo for help lowering the heavy gurney out of the ambulance. Then either because he sensed or smelled his favorite human, Tag wrenched loose from Binney. In a single bound he set his paws on the rolling bed's metal frame and amid happy yelps proceeded to lick Rio's ear and face.

"Whoa, whoa. Hold it, Tagalong!" Rio scrunched up his face, but he couldn't escape the swath of the long pink tongue the way he was strapped down and hampered from moving his head aside by the cervical collar.

"I'm so sorry I lost my hold on him." Horrified, Binney rushed over to again try to curb Rio's enthusiastic pet.

"Binney, thanks for grabbing him. Tag is just happy to see me. But he's on my wrong side, my bad side, so I can't even pet him."

A thundering horse rounded the corner of the house. Rio's ranch hand yanked hard on the reins of the powerful palomino, stopping short of the gurney and the shocked men trying to shield their patient from another onslaught. Binney clamped both hands around Tag's collar, but she couldn't drag his feet down from his master's arm.

JJ Montoya vaulted off his mount's bare back, removed his stained cowboy hat and shoved the big horse back a few steps. "Geez, Rio. I had Buttercup's colt on a lunge line in the arena behind the barn. I totally lost track of time until Tag bolted and cleared the fence. By the time it dawned on me where he was headed, I had to release the colt and toss a bridle on Nugget here. Tagalong, heel," he ordered. "He didn't hurt you, did he?" JJ asked as the dog acted confused, but did drop to his belly, tugging Binney along as he flopped across JJ's boots.

The ambulance driver took the opportunity to signal to Jorge, who still braced the foot of the rolling gurney. "Let's get Mr. McNabb into the house before any other animals show up. Delivering him safely is our obligation. We'll let his nurse and the other guy sort out the menagerie."

"I'll have to unlock the front door," JJ announced. "Ms. Taylor…that's right, isn't it? Can you hang on to Tag and steady Nugget?" He dug a key ring out of his jeans pocket.

"Is the hospital bed you rented prepared and set up to receive Rio?" she called to the man charging up the porch steps.

He turned and moved aside to let the men maneuver their patient up to the porch. "The rental bed came with a sheet and pillow. I opened it up but just set it in the middle of the living room. I'd better come spell you, so you and Rio can decide where you want it moved." He unlocked and opened the house door.

She sighed as he jogged back and took over animal control. "It's up to Rio where he wants to spend the majority of his days and nights for a while. It'd be nice to have an area with a lot of natural light. However, for your convenience," she said, pausing next to Rio, "with as few steps as possible to at least a three-quarter bathroom."

"Then the living room, but toward the back patio. Anywhere, really. I'm just damned glad to be home." Rio gestured with his hand not confined in a cast. "When my folks remodeled, they added a bath by the patio doors so people coming in from the pool or the gardens could change clothes or shower."

"Perfect." Binney hurried inside, quickly took measure of the room then dragged the rental bed toward a set of sliding glass doors. "It really is perfect," she said to the men following her. "Setting his bed here gives me a choice of chairs to use where I can keep an eye on him. And this way the bathroom is on the side of his uninjured leg."

Jorge locked down the wheels on the rental then he and Leo moved Rio off the portable.

Binney made sure he was comfortable before pulling up the side rails.

"What's that on your back?" Rio asked when she turned to thank the men and walk them out. "A guitar? You play guitar?"

She made a face. "Play is a stretch. More like plunk around on it. My neighbor said I should bring it and claims she likes my music. But she's almost ninety so is likely hard of hearing." Sliding the strap off her shoulder, she set the case by the door.

"I have an electronic keyboard in my travel trailer. You could say I plunk around, too. Sometimes Tagalong likes my tunes. Sometimes he growls, and I swear he puts his paws over his ears." Rio cracked a smile. "How long do you suppose it will be until I get this cast removed so I have use of my fingers again?"

"Did no one provide you with follow-up instructions before you checked out?"

"Come to think of it, Dr. Darnell folded some papers into an envelope he tucked under my pillow. He wants X-rays in three weeks. The good news is that he said by then I might be able to get in and out of JJ's pickup for the ride to the lab."

"I'll find the envelope in a minute. I want to run out and get my saddlebags with my clothes and miscellaneous medical supplies. Shall I ask if JJ wants to come in to talk to you for a few minutes? I see he's still standing out there holding his horse and Tag. I imagine he's waiting for the ambulance to leave."

"He can come in anytime. Will you bring Tag in? He's used to being with me unless I rode in a rodeo event. Then he was confined to my trailer. I hope he won't keep on acting upset about not being able to climb up on this bed. I suppose you'll say it's wrong how I share my bed with the mutt."

"Not up to me to judge. Pure curiosity," she said from the doorway, "How does your girlfriend feel about that? Tag's a pretty big dog."

"Girlfriend?" Rio gave a belly laugh. "It's been three years since anyone even remotely fit that description. And I honestly can't recall if she ever met Tagalong."

"My mistake." Binney opened the door, but Rio's next statement stopped her.

"To call something a mistake insinuates you had reason to believe such a person exists. Or are you fishing?"

Swamped by old feelings she hadn't navigated in years, Binney's breath hitched. "One of the ward nurses said your girlfriend visited you in the hospital. I frankly have no reason to care one way or the other since you're just my patient," she said, digging up a grin. But she lost her hold on the screen door and it slammed, leaving her unfinished thought trailing in the air while she completed her exit from the house.

RIO'S JAW FLEXED hard enough to radiate pain down his neck. He knew he shouldn't be developing feelings for her, but some had sneaked in. As she'd plainly admitted that she'd once hoped to date his twin, he wondered if that interest also stood as a barrier between them. If that were the case he needed to back off. There had always been rivalry between Ryder and him even though everyone tended to think they were alike. Nothing could be further from the truth.

Damn, now he wondered if the nurse he needed for the duration of his incapacitation maybe accepted this job hoping Ryder might drop in on him so they could reconnect. The possibility disappointed him and caused a hole to crater in his chest. Should he tell her that wasn't bloody likely?

JJ had told him he sometimes imagined slights and blew innocent remarks out of proportion. Was that what he was doing with Binney?

Thinking of his ranch hand, in he walked with Tag bounding ahead, and Binney at his heels. So if she was always around it'd be a long time before Rio would get the chance to voice his question to JJ.

It was JJ who directed Binney to the guest room she'd use while staying at the Lonesome Road. That, too, left Rio feeling helpless and useless.

He could see into her room as she'd left the bedroom door open. As a result he kept his conversation with JJ strictly on ranch matters.

"Why all of these orders suddenly? You haven't been gone from the ranch as long as you sometimes are at rodeos, Rio. Nothing's changed. My workload is the same unless you buy that pregnant mare from the guy out of Pecos." JJ snapped his fingers. "That reminds me. Here's a check from the local rodeo association. Seems a bunch of people who witnessed your accident contributed in your name to the benevolence fund." Unsnapping the pearl button on his shirt pocket, JJ extracted a folded check. He read off a sum that had Rio whistling through his teeth.

"Should I accept it? I'm not down-and-out like some guys who get hurt."

"The note said this money was given in your name. And you do have hospital bills."

"True. Did they include a list of people who donated?" Rio asked. "I should send thank-you notes. My orthopedic doc said I can sit in my recliner every day to use that electronic device he says will help heal my cracked vertebrae. Unless it clashes with our Wi-Fi or something in my laptop, maybe I can type notes with one hand and you can print them off and get 'em in the mail."

"I don't know diddly-squat about how to even turn on your printer." JJ made a face. "Maybe Rhonda can operate your setup. Or Nurse Taylor," he added when she reentered the living room.

"What about Nurse Taylor?" she asked.

JJ started to apprise her of what he'd said, but Rio interrupted. "She's only here to take care of my medical needs. There's no reason for her to mess in ranch business."

"Well, *excuse* me," JJ strung out, climbing to his

feet. "I assumed she'd have to help in the office, too, since you're stove-up."

The dog, who'd flopped down between Rio's bed and JJ, lumbered up and over to Binney, nudging her until she rubbed his ears.

Pursing his lips, JJ stomped past her and on out of the house.

Approaching a sour-looking Rio, Binney asked lightly, "What was that all about?"

"Nothing. He…just…nothing!"

She arched an eyebrow. "Okay. It's time for your afternoon pain pill. If you point me to the kitchen I can bring you water to take it with, or make some iced tea. I brought tea bags in case you don't stock those."

"I do." Rio released a sigh. "I owe JJ an apology. I just snapped at him and said you were here only to take care of my medical needs. Obviously I need you to handle other things, such as…" He waved the check. "I hate to ask, by chance can you make a deposit to my ranch account, and help print off thank-you notes if I'm able to type them?"

"Probably. I presume you bank in town. Was JJ objecting to taking it there? Just so you know it will be at least a week until I'm comfortable leaving you alone."

"I bank online. JJ claims he can't work our computer."

"Do you know Bob Foster? When his wife was laid up after surgery, I took care of her, their home, prepared meals and handled their ranch bookkeeping on a computer."

"Great." Rio pointed to an archway with the flopping check. "Kitchen's that way. I'd like iced tea. Until it's brewed I'll phone JJ and mend fences. I'll have him bring my laptop from the office and we'll deposit this later."

Binney smiled and squeezed Rio's wrist. "I like a man who's willing to admit that he needs to say he's sorry."

She left the room and Rio glanced down where he fancied he still felt her warm touch. The thing he was sorriest about but couldn't admit to her was that his brother stood like a brick wall between them.

Chapter Five

"You have a dream kitchen," Binney said, returning a short time later with Rio's iced tea and his pain pill, and Tag not letting her out of his sight. "It opens out into the most fantastic screened patio. Do you entertain a lot?" She placed the pill in his unbandaged hand and elevated the electronically operated upper bed while still holding his tumbler of tea so it wouldn't spill.

Rio took the pill and swallowed it down with her assistance. He gave a dry laugh. "JJ's fiancée says I only have a kitchen because it came with the house." He drank more tea. "This hits the spot. But in ten minutes it's gonna need to hit you-know-what. I guess we'll soon see if the two of us can get me into the john."

Setting the glass down, she let him lean back against the pillows again then spared a moment to study the room. "This Saltillo tiled floor makes for easy walking. We don't have as far to go as you did in the hospital." She made the trek herself and peered in the bathroom before returning to his side. "Nice,

Rio. With that large, walk-in shower you have plenty of room for me to help you get in and out, dried off and dressed."

He screwed up his face and she took his hand. "Are you fighting modesty again? Think of me as a robot, not a woman."

His grating half laugh revealed what he thought of that notion. "Maybe if you wore feed sacks from head to toe." He broke off talking as she picked up the glass and once more offered him a drink.

He could get used to having her support his head and neck. And he loved the play of the afternoon sun shining through the tall sliding glass doors to burnish Binney's smooth skin. A bright beam left her short red-blond curls a fiery halo.

His mouth suddenly dry, and other parts of his body reacting, Rio blindly reached his uninjured hand out for the glass, or her, but the clavicle brace restrained him and pain caused him to miss the glass, drop his arm and howl.

Binney hurriedly bent over him, concern carving lines around her mouth. "No sudden moves, Rio. For at least the next couple of weeks you have to speak up and ask me for anything you want." She held the glass to his lips and lightly rubbed between his shoulder blades as he drank his fill.

"You have magic hands. I'm positive no robot matches that. And," he added, "in the sunlight you look like an angel."

Gaze tripping lightly over his earnest face, Binney shook her head. In a no-nonsense voice she said, "No flirting with your nurse allowed. I know that's how you and Ryder cut wide swaths through the female population in high school. Very probably through female rodeo fans, as well. We learn in nursing school to be immune to flattery."

"But you weren't immune in high school. You've said as much. On the other hand if it's true you never dated Ryder, it's hard for me to believe." He deliberately eyed her up and down. "Ryder brags that he dated every pretty girl in the county and left them heartbroken after he dropped them—which he always did." Rio brightened. "Are you trying to tell me you're the exception even though you admitted you wanted to go out with him?"

"Stop it!" Binney stepped away from his bed, set the glass down again and rubbed her upper arms. "If you must know, Ryder asked me to one of the school dances. He never came to pick me up, nor did he bother to call and cancel. Other girls delighted in telling me he'd taken Samantha Walker to the dance instead."

Rio stared at her. "I can't imagine why he would've done that."

Binney's laugh was brittle. "Yet you didn't even remember that we went to the same school. Much of your crowd probably never knew I existed. Those who did looked down on me because I started life as an abandoned baby. I wasn't adopted, and I bounced around foster homes. There may be loving foster families, kind of like how you've cared for and adopted a foundling dog. I was never more than a pair of extra work hands for my foster folks. At sixteen I asked to live in the Catholic group home. I still had chores, but also time to study and take a paying job at a nursing home. It let me save money to attend college. Now you see why someone like your brother wouldn't feel a need to call and dump me."

"I'm sorry. I'll apologize for Ryder. I know he had his pick of girls, but still…"

"You act as if he was an anomaly. You had your share of adulation. Back then the majority of girls didn't distinguish between you two."

"And yet you did," Rio noted, sounding disgruntled. "At least at the hospital you said it was Ryder you worshipped from afar."

"Did I? Since I was applying to be your employee it would've been unseemly to suggest anything different. May I ask now for a big favor? Can we put this pointless line of discussion to rest? High school was ages ago. Life goes on. People mature. I certainly did, and I'm in your orbit for one reason. To help you recover from a bad accident. Can we agree on that?"

His gaze slowly cruised over her from head to foot and back again for a while. His ultimate response was little more than a grunt.

"I'll take that as a yes." She helped him finish the tea before asking in a normal tone, "What sounds appetizing for supper? You know better than I what's stocked in your kitchen."

"I don't have any idea what's left from last time I was home. Rhonda, that's JJ's fiancée, has a key.

She comes in after I leave for a rodeo to clean out my fridge."

"I haven't seen a woman around. Does she live on the ranch?"

"She rents a place in town near where she works. Weekends she spends in JJ's house here on the property. If I leave anything they can use, she's free to take it. Otherwise she bags it for the trash that gets picked up out on the main road every Thursday. All I know is I'd like some real food instead of that hospital crap."

Binney set the empty tea glass on a small table near Rio's bed. Tag bounced eagerly up.

Feeling around under Rio's pillow where he'd said Dr. Darnell had tucked an envelope with discharge instructions, she found it and extracted a page. "This says you can gradually get back to a normal diet and taper off opiates. Suzette gave me enough pain pills to last you today and tomorrow. And a script for another week."

"That's the pill you just gave me? I assume so since I'm already feeling loosey-goosey. I prefer to switch ASAP to whatever over-the-counter pills are in the medicine cabinet in my private john. Before you go find it, will you help me to the closest one?" He started to move on his own and rattled the bed rail.

"Hold on a minute." Binney dropped the paper she'd been reading, snatched up one crutch JJ had set by the bed and quickly let down the rail. "Easy does it. I intended to find you real clothes to put on at your first excursion. As that requires altering your jeans, we'll do that tomorrow. Do you have pajamas someplace that I can get?"

"I...uh...no. I sleep in my underwear."

"Ah."

"Can we hurry? But don't let me slip."

"You're still wearing the slipper socks they gave you at the hospital." Binney secured an arm around his waist, lowered the electric bed and helped him stand. "You're really wobbly. Next time, make this trek prior to getting a pain pill."

He leaned more heavily against her slight frame. "We can solve that by stopping the damn things." His sharp response had Tag whining in concern.

"Tag, sit," Rio ordered.

"I've heard that big talk about quitting painkillers before," Binney said, carefully navigating past the dog, who'd sat as Rio directed. "I want you to cut back, too, but not until your pain is tolerable." They entered the bathroom and he immediately told her to leave.

She blew out an exasperated sigh. "Sit your ass down and quit being one." She guided him to the commode.

"You sound tough, but I'm the boss. Now out."

Ignoring him she eyed the glassed-in shower. "It's going to get old fast if we have this fight every time you need to pee or shower. Ward nurses said you liked lotion rubdowns before bed. Nothing's different here."

"There's a lot different," he fumed. "Those nurses

were my mom's age. They've all raised kids. Unlike you, I figure they'd all powdered a lot of bottoms. Now out. Please," he begged, gazing at Binney with pleading, pewter eyes.

"Okay. I'll step outside the door. But I'm telling you straight, if you fall off the pot, I'm calling an ambulance to take you straight to Baxter Rehab. Unless you do damage enough to need to go back to the ICU."

WAITING IMPATIENTLY OUTSIDE the door, Binney rubbed Tag's ears. He'd scooted up to her on his belly. She did take pity on Rio. His feelings weren't anything new. Younger men often requested older nurses. In San Antonio where she'd trained, many male patients came from the oil fields, agriculture or ranches. Those types frequently objected to young trainees. It took her a while to realize their qualms had little to do with her not yet having an RN on her name tag. Supervisors joked that youthful nurses should buy gray wigs and granny glasses.

She heard the toilet flush, peeked in and was stunned to see Rio standing up, balancing on one foot, bracing his hips against the sink while he washed the hand not in a cast.

"All right. You've proved you're gutsy. But let's get you back to your bed before you run out of gas," she said, bursting in to wrap an arm around him again.

He treated her to a winsome smile. "I swear I'm feeling better. Maybe simply because I'm home. Any chance you can rummage in my closet and get me some of those real clothes?"

"Sure, I guess. Gosh, those pills usually knock you for a loop," she said as she settled them hip to hip and guided him across the room. "Once you're in bed you can tell me what to fetch and where."

"Shirts and jeans in the closet. Underwear in the top dresser drawer. I'll put those on by myself, but you'll have to help with the jeans."

"Where will I find scissors to rip out a seam?" She eased him down onto his bed, but he seemed reluctant to let go of her.

"I have wire cutters out in the barn," he said cheekily.

"Great. I think I have a small pair of scissors I brought to cut tape."

"Tape?" Rio's eyelids fluttered and closed as Binney slipped loose and engaged the bed rail.

"Yes, I have to tape plastic wrap around your cast and your cervical collar each time you shower. I brought a second clavicle brace we can trade out while one dries."

"You know best." He punctuated that with a yawn.

"I'll go see what I can find for you to put on. Then I have to get something started for supper."

Rio didn't answer. Binney noticed he'd fallen fast asleep. She smiled down on him, and murmured, "Zonked. Come on, Tag. Let's go see what we can find to eat. He won't be ready to have those clothes for a couple of hours. And you, my friend, are probably hungry and thirsty, too. I hate to rummage through Rio's cupboards, but I don't know any other way to find what we need." She went into the kitchen and Tag followed. He padded across the tile and sat in front of two ceramic bowls, both were licked clean.

Binney chose one and filled it with water. Tag immediately woofed and bent his head to lap up the contents.

She opened a cupboard that might be a pantry and was rewarded with shelves of canned goods. Two bags of kibble sat on the floor. One was open and held a scoop. Only guessing, because she'd never owned a pet, she dumped two scoops of pellets into Tag's second bowl.

He gave her a damp lick of her hand, which she accepted as a happy response. When she returned the kibble sack to the pantry she scanned the shelves and found several boxes of macaroni and cheese. "Perfect for Rio," she muttered. She also discovered bread mixes, and on the counter a bread machine exactly like one she owned. Pleased, she washed her hands and hummed while preparing the dough and setting the maker to rise and bake the herb loaf.

Seeming replete, Tag stayed glued to her side.

"It's time to go find your master some clothes," she said, marveling at how quickly she'd begun talking to the animal as if he were human. Oddly, as if he understood, he led the way to Rio's bedroom.

Tag jumped up and lay on the foot of the big bed. *Giant bed*, Binney thought, judging there'd be room for three people and the lanky dog to sleep side by side.

Feeling guilty for having any such thoughts about an employer's bed, she went to a tall dresser and in the top drawer as Rio had indicated sat stacks of white briefs and cotton undershirts. She left the shirts, considering it wasn't cold even in the air-conditioned home.

She felt a bit uncomfortable opening a closet that wasn't hers, but compared to a couple of ranchers she'd worked for, Rio's closet was neat. She selected a chambray short-sleeved shirt and a pair of worn jeans.

Although it felt nosy, it was difficult to not check out his bedroom. What struck her first was a lack of anything on the taupe-colored walls. His dresser and nightstands were also devoid of anything personal like family photos. Two lamps and an alarm clock left her a bit sad to think of anyone's life this barren. Especially a man she knew for a fact had grown up in what she'd always heard was a caring family.

Leaving the room after Tag hopped off the bed to join her, she scrolled back in her mind to a time she had cut shots of families out of magazines and carried them in her wallet just to pretend she had folks who loved her. She no longer did anything so pathetic, but reflecting on Rio's bedroom she thought about all the framed prints on her walls. She had knickknacks, too, and baskets of dried flowers. Stuff in home-goods stores that she'd seen moms with children buy. Family was an area in her life with hurtful gaps, still incomplete. Yet she still dreamed big.

She pictured one day having a loving husband and three or four kids.

In the living room, her patient slept on. Feeling domestic she got out her scissors, ripped the seam out of one pant leg almost to the knee so it would go over his bubble-wrapped injured foot and ankle. Afterward she set his clothing in one of the recliners and curled up in the other with one of many ranch magazines tucked in a rack attached to a floor lamp.

Tag nosed his way up on her lap and attempted to make himself a lap dog. Binney scooted to one side to give him more room. Laughing softly so as not to wake Rio, she hugged Tag and kissed him between his furry ears. Then lifting her head, her gaze lit on Rio. His almost black hair had a lot of natural curl she hadn't noticed before. Even sporting the scruff he'd shaved off once in the hospital, he was still darned fine-looking. His high cheekbones, straight nose and narrow jaw with the slightest cleft in his chin presented too much of an enticing picture.

She forced her focus back on the article about cattle ranchers who loved the land in beautiful but rugged places. She wondered if that applied to horse ranchers, too. Probably so. She imagined the hard work and long solitary days that must be a part of life out here on the Lonesome Road.

Before she could find another short read, the bread machine dinged, letting her know the bread she'd been able to smell for a while was done. Hating to disturb Tag, who'd also gone to sleep, she nevertheless needed to rescue the loaf.

She roused the dog and he trailed her to the kitchen, where she washed her hands and brought the round out to cool. There was butter in the fridge. And she'd set out a pot to fix the macaroni and cheese. It wouldn't take long to throw supper together once Rio woke up.

Going back to the living room Tag again settled on her lap. She picked up her magazine and chanced to see Rio open his eyes. For an elongated moment he gazed at her as if confused to see her seated in his recliner.

She witnessed the slow lifting of his fog. His slightly off-kilter, sweet smile that followed sent her heartbeat drumming in her chest.

"FYI," he said. "Tag's a bed hog. Since these bed rails won't let him jump up here with me, don't be surprised if he sleeps with you tonight."

"I don't mind. Unless you object. I mean, will that play havoc with his training?"

"I haven't really trained him. I admit I'm surprised by how fast he took to you."

"Gee, thanks."

"I didn't mean that disparagingly. It's that JJ claims Tag whines and stays by their front door the few times I've had to leave him at their cottage overnight."

"I was teasing."

Rio suddenly sniffed the air. "Something smells good. Did you fix supper? Whatever it is makes my stomach growl."

"I baked herb bread." Binney moved Tag and

stood up. "I fed Tag. Guessed at giving him two scoops of dry food. I plan to make mac and cheese to go with the bread if it sounds okay to you. I'll bring you a plate and set up the bed's tray table. Tomorrow, after you shower and put on the clothes I found, we'll see if you can sit at the kitchen table to eat breakfast."

"I'm ready to try that now. And Tag gets three scoops of kibble." He pushed the button and raised the head of his bed.

"I'll give him another to chow down on while I fix supper. Rio, I know you want to jump straight into your old life. Dr. Darnell's notes say to go slow. In the morning we'll see how you tolerate sitting on the shower bench. Like at the hospital, it will require finessing around your casted hand, neck collar and cervical brace. The former I'll cover with plastic wrap. The latter we'll let get wet and change out when you're done. Likewise I'll remove the Ace wrap on your leg and restore it after you dry off."

"Yeah, I know I'm anxious to be well." He tried to touch his face, but his arm was restricted by the support clipped to the clavicle brace. "Damn, how's a guy supposed to eat? Or shave? My face itches under these whiskers."

"Patience. I can relax the brace provided your back is fully supported by the bed or eventually we'll try one of these recliners. You can shave yourself if you have an electric razor."

"I do in my bathroom. It probably needs charging."

"I'll take care of that." She left the room, un-earthed it in his bathroom and plugged it in. "That's done," she said as she returned. "I'm going to feed Tag more, then cook our meal. So don't foolishly try to lower the bed and get out without assistance."

"You'd make a good military drill sergeant. How did you end up in nursing?"

"How did you end up a patient? You found some-thing you loved to do and were good at. Loving horses and riding. For me it's liking to see people be hale and hearty, and being good at caring for them when they're not."

Binney reached the kitchen archway expecting a comeback. As she left the living room he still hadn't said anything. A quick glance back showed his eyes trained on her, steady and somber, but with an added expression she couldn't name. She had no idea what he was thinking, but she maybe ought to avoid fur-ther verbal sparring.

She returned twenty minutes later, and he'd fallen asleep again.

"Rio," she called softly. "I have your supper."

He blinked awake.

"I need to balance this tray on your lap and raise you into a sitting position. Then I'll unhook the support so you have greater motion with your good arm." She went through the steps methodically, giv-ing him time to adjust to each.

"Comfort food," he said after savoring his first bite. "Did you already eat?"

"I'll have mine later. This is more solid food than

you ate in the hospital. I want to be handy in case you have trouble swallowing."

"Your food will get cold. I'm fine. Go dish up a plate."

"You have a microwave. I can warm something up later."

"Quit being stubborn. I hate eating alone."

She threw up her hands. "Who's stubborn? You want me to stand by your bed and eat my supper?"

"There's room on my tray. And you can drag over a bar stool."

"Okay, but don't you dare choke while I'm gone."

He shot her a toothy smile. "Patient one. Nurse nothing."

"Is everything a competition with you?" she grumbled. Her query didn't get an answer until she returned carrying her plate, and pulled over a bar stool.

"I had to think on your last question about competition. Frankly I'm surprised, but maybe you're right. I am pretty competitive."

"I suppose that comes from all the time you've spent bronc riding." She broke a piece off her bread and ate it slowly.

"Actually I think it goes back to the cradle. Or the womb. You're a nurse. Have you seen evidence of sparring in ultrasounds of twins?"

She laughed. "Not that I recall." She watched Rio scoop in several forkfuls of mac and cheese. "I only did one rotation in OB, but you've brought up an interesting theory about competition and twins. I have my laptop. I'll do some research online. What did you two compete over?"

"Everything. From toys, to cupcakes, to boots, to…" He chewed his bread and gazed into the distance before he swallowed then admitted, "…horses, and even friends." Their eyes met and he added with fervor, "I can assure you that if I'd been the one to ask you to a dance, I'd have taken you come hell or high water."

Binney's mouth fell open at hearing his last pronouncement. "Uh, I have to say in high school anytime I passed either of you, you were in a circle of other popular kids."

Rio stopped eating. "To me, high school and early rodeo weren't fun. My brother had to win or he'd pitch a fit."

"I always thought you were best friends. Certainly you were both popular and both excelled at sports." She idly dragged a fork through her food. "I would've loved having a sibling of any age. I hope you and Ryder have put petty envy behind you."

He shrugged. "The past four years we've gone our separate ways."

"So you don't own the Lonesome Road together?"

"No. He says he hated this backwater spot. If you're hoping he'll drop by, it's not gonna happen. He's gone for good."

She frowned then rolled her eyes. "The only reason I might hope such a thing, Rio, is that you're injured. I should think a visit by family would mean a lot. Will your folks visit?"

"They're vacationing in Australia. I hope they don't get wind of my accident. This trip is something Mom's wanted forever." He polished off his mac and cheese and sank back against his pillows.

"You seem distressed. Are you in pain? I don't want you to lie flat this soon after eating, but you've sat up fairly straight for quite a while. Let me clear away our plates and ease the head of your bed into more of an incline."

"You're still eating. I'm okay. We can talk about something else. I'm not big on revisiting my past."

"That surprises me." She started to ask what could possibly be bothersome about what she'd always judged the McNabb twins' storybook life to be like, but there was a sharp rap at the door.

Binney scrambled off the stool and quickly gathered their plates. She set them aside and rushed toward the door only to see it open, and JJ and a gorgeous woman with long black hair walked in. They were loaded down with grocery sacks.

"We got here too late to fix you supper," the woman said, sniffing the air. "I'm Rhonda Lopez, JJ's fiancée," she added, smiling at Binney. "I know your name, and that you're Rio's private nurse. After JJ explained the extent of Rio's injuries, I told him we needed to pick up supplies. Shall we take these to the kitchen and chat while the men discuss horsey stuff?" Rhonda quickly turned to JJ. "Be nice. Tell Rio not to worry about the bookkeeping. If I can't figure out the ranch system, my sister works at a bank and I'll ask for her help."

Rio gestured with his good hand. "It's settled. I left a message on your house phone, JJ. Binney handled Bob Foster's ranch accounts. But gosh, guys, thanks for the supplies. While you're here, JJ, let's discuss that pregnant mare we talked about buying."

"Give me a minute to adjust the head of Rio's bed," Binney said, brushing past the other man. "He's sat up long enough. You two can still talk if he lies back a bit." In a few short strokes she'd straightened his bedding, fluffed his pillows and let the bed down halfway from what it'd been. "Better?" she asked, deftly refastening the loose strap on his clavicle brace.

Even if he hadn't sent Binney a smile that reached his eyes and lingered on her through several heartbeats, his expelled breath would have conveyed his relief. Going one better, he caught her hand before she slipped away. "Just so we're clear, hiring you is the smartest thing I've done recently."

Sensing his friends' curious expressions trained on her, she tucked her chin down. "I…ah…hope you're still of the same mind once I start getting you up and about two or three times a day." Freeing herself, she backed away from the bed and took the sacks JJ still held.

The dog seemed unsure who to follow. He ended up flopping down between where JJ sat on the empty bar stool and Rio's bed.

In the silence that fell over the room, Binney's boot heels clicked loudly on the tile floor as she zipped into the kitchen behind JJ's fiancée.

Thankfully, Rhonda didn't probe into what that last exchange had been all about. But she mentioned not remembering Binney from high school.

"You probably wouldn't if we didn't have any classes together. I worked after school, and never took part in any extracurricular activities." Binney opened the pantry and they began unloading groceries.

"Makes sense, then." Rhonda carried one sack to the refrigerator. "We bought standard supplies." She took out eggs, milk and cheese. "The only meat we picked up was hamburger. Although JJ says Rio complained about not being able to eat steak, from the sound of his injuries I wasn't sure he could cut steak." After closing the fridge door, Rhonda folded bags together.

"He'll work up to a regular diet once he's up and around more. The doctor had him on a soft diet because of his collapsed lung."

The other woman winced. "JJ says he's never seen Rio hurt this bad."

"Rhonda? Are you ready to leave?" JJ called from the arch.

"Yes, I think we're finished here." Turning to Binney, she said, "Anything else you need from the store or anywhere, tell JJ."

Binney impulsively hugged the other woman. "I appreciate having milk and eggs for morning." She straightened and murmured to JJ, who'd come into the kitchen. "I'd like to surprise Rio with a wheelchair if you can swing it. He'd benefit from getting out in the sun. You can find one with outdoor tires where you rented the bed."

"Sure thing. I can pick it up when I go to Pecos after the mare Rio's buying. I know he's already antsy to see the new horse I'm set to pick up next week. Think you can wheel him out to a corral by next Thursday or Friday?"

"We can shoot for that." The three walked back into the living room. "Our first order of business is bathing, shaving and sitting for a treatment with the TENS. By the way," Binney continued, "these recliners are soft. Any chance we can come up with a wooden rocking chair?"

Hearing them, Rio hollered from his bed. "Any chance I can get a shower and shave tonight? Twist JJ's arm to stick around and help me."

Binney almost laughed at the ranch hand's visible panic. "It's really not hard. He doesn't want me to see him naked," she confided. "Would you mind assisting tonight? He'll get over his modesty in time. But a shower tonight will be beneficial."

Rhonda excused herself to Binney and waved goodbye to Rio. "I'll see you at the cottage," she told JJ, and the two brushed lips.

Binney felt the love radiating between the pair and her heart lurched with envy. Detouring to the door that led to Rio's bedroom, she addressed JJ, "I'll bring his robe and slippers. You can help him shave while I set up for his shower."

THE MEN HAD Rio clean-shaven when she later emerged from his bedroom. JJ had rolled up his shirtsleeves. He and Binney jockeyed Rio out of bed.

After they walked him to the bathroom, one on either side, she got out the plastic wrap to keep Rio's cast dry. "Once he's showered and you have him dry and in his briefs, JJ, we'll take him back to bed. I'll remove the plastic wrap and rub on lotion designed to stave off bedsores." Smiling at Rio, she added, "Then we'll get you into a fresh clavicle brace and restore the ankle and foot wrap."

"What about my shirt and jeans? Won't JJ already have me in those?"

Binney taped the last of the plastic around his casted hand. "Trust me. I have loads of experience dressing stubborn guys like you."

JJ laughed. "We men are the opposite. We're good at undressing you gals."

Rio scowled at his friend. The minute Binney had finished wrapping the plastic, he was plainly anxious for her to go.

Hovering outside the bathroom along with Tagalong, she blocked out the men's chatter and listened as the shower went on and the shower door closed. Subsequent sessions would get easier. The first one at home for a patient was most difficult. Especially for a male patient who had a female nurse. Some never let go of their modesty. She hoped Rio could.

It seemed a long time after the water shut off that JJ summoned her. "I'm going home. He's all yours," the very wet man stated. He was out the front door before Binney could say goodbye.

"I'm worn out," Rio fretted. "Can we just get the rest of my clothes on so I can go to sleep?"

Binney tucked the single crutch under his bare arm and slipped her arm around his damp waist. "I'll be quick with the lotion. Move, Tag," she told the dog.

It took them a while to make it across to the bed, where Rio sank back with a groan.

Totally unprepared to experience a punch in her gut from merely looking at him sprawled on his bed in nothing but briefs, lotion she usually warmed between her hands sizzled. Averting her eyes, she started at his feet and worked up his legs, and felt his slumberous gaze track her every move. A duty that normally didn't feel intimate to her, suddenly did.

Privately she chanted a mantra over and over. *You're a nurse. He's a patient. You're a nurse. He's a patient.*

One fine-looking patient who showed by his grin that he'd begun to enjoy the whole process way too much as she smoothed lotion over nicely rippled muscles along his lower abs and his manly chest.

Chapter Six

Almost two weeks after his first night at home, Rio's life had settled into a comfortable routine. Every day that passed he'd grown more at ease having Binney around helping him, cooking for him, talking with him, laughing together, playing guitar for him and. yes, he thought, running her soft hands and warm lotion over most of his body. His heart kicked over and his chest tingled as he lay there imagining it. He'd started dreaming about her when he slept. That was new for him.

Midweek JJ had hauled in the wooden rocker Binney had requested. Its seat and back cushions were made of foam and yet the chair was sturdy enough to support his back when Binney hooked him up to the TENS Unit. He didn't know if the treatments he took twice a day were helping his neck. Binney said they'd find out when he had his X-ray the following week. They both came to realize that he wasn't good at being idle. Binney brought in his electronic keyboard. He could only make music with one hand, but

Rio relaxed more when they laughingly made bad music together.

Today she'd gone outside after lunch and had taken Tag. As a rule she didn't hike to the end of the lane for mail until later in the day. But she and the dog hadn't yet returned. Her lengthy absence let Rio's restless mind travel a meandering path. He couldn't say when he'd started missing her if she wasn't around, but now he wondered exactly what that meant. Did it mean she'd gotten under his skin? He definitely felt a growing closeness toward her. He thought…hoped…she shared his feelings.

Silent though the house was, his musings were interrupted and his attention diverted to a commotion coming from outside at the front of the house. A loud engine. Gravel spewing. And Tag barking up a storm.

That's when Rio remembered JJ had gone to Pecos to buy the new mare.

He chafed, wishing he could get out of bed to go see the horse he'd spent his money on. *Why couldn't he?* His crutch was within reach if he shifted his butt and grabbed the handrail with his good hand. Oh, but how many times had Binney cautioned him to wait for help? Too many times to count. However, before she'd always been within calling distance.

Yesterday she'd said he was moving better. In fact he'd walked alone from his bed to the rocking chair. And she really only guided him to and from the bathroom. Once there he shaved, showered, dried off and tugged on sweatpants she'd had JJ pick up at the store.

Man, he hated being dependent. If he didn't start taking some initiative, wouldn't his muscles go to hell?

Doubling down on a determination to show he could be more independent, he managed to drop the side rail and swing his legs around. That was a mistake. He realized at once the move would land him on his bum ankle. Plus, the crutch now stood where he'd need to grab it with his casted hand.

In attempting to roll over on his belly to rectify the problem, his lower body and legs dangled half on, half off the bed. That's when the front door flew open with a bang. A sound that made him jerk, which shot pain up his spine.

He heard Tag lope across the tile, his toenails tapping loudly until he leaped up and hit Rio in the butt with both his feet. "Dammit!" Rio couldn't see what was happening to make all that rattling at the door.

All too soon there was no mistaking the panic in Binney's voice when she yelped, "Rio, what in heaven's name are you doing?"

Giving up, he lay still, and was glad when she shooed Tag away and he soon felt her secure grip steering him to his feet. Her hands were touching him, magically but dependably.

"I heard JJ drive in. I figured if I could make it to the porch he might stop and let me see Contessa."

"Who?" Binney gathered him close and turned him until he bore his weight on his good leg.

"That's the mare we acquired. I've only seen her photo and read up on her bloodline and that of the stallion to whom she was bred. All of that is essential to retaining a pure palomino registry. Nearly as important to me is how well she shows. How she holds her head. JJ's the best when it comes to weaning and breaking stock, but I have a sixth sense when it comes to choosing horseflesh."

"Well, then, I have a nice surprise for you." Binney tucked his crutch under his arm and moved him in a circle. "I shouldn't reward you for bad behavior," she scolded and gave him a little shake. "If you'd fallen it would've set back what progress you've made. And you scared me. Can you feel my heart pounding?"

He could, but it wasn't bad in his estimation. Still, he bit his upper lip between his teeth. "I know. I'm sorry."

She brightened again. "Because you've done so well, I thought you deserved a treat. I asked JJ to pick up a wheelchair. Ta da!" She pointed to where Tag sat thumping his tail on the floor as if also eagerly awaiting his master's reaction.

Rio let out an excited whoop. He squeezed Binney tight and awkwardly dropped a kiss on top of her head. "I think I love you," he blurted. "I've been dying to see the horses, and get out around the ranch. Let's go. What are we waiting for?"

His oh-so-casual declaration of love rattled Binney even though she knew it didn't mean a thing. And yet, hearing words she used to long for someone to say and mean, but no one ever had, welded her feet to the floor.

"Come on. Come on. What's wrong, Binney? I didn't hurt you, did I? I forget this cast on my hand and wrist isn't soft." He loosened his hold a bit.

The dog dropped down and whined.

"I'm fine," she assured Rio and calmed her giddy equilibrium. "Okay, so if the wheelchair runs well on gravel, we can get you outside for a while every day." Escorting him the short distance to the chair, she bent and locked the wheels. It took muscle to balance him so he didn't sit too fast.

"Why wouldn't it run on gravel?"

His face seemed all too close to hers. Their eyes locked and felt like a soft caress. Trembling, Binney jerked back and almost fell over Tagalong.

"Hey, hey. Careful." Rio grabbed her forearm. "Ah, damn. I only realized we, uh…you, have to get me and this contraption off the porch. There're only three steps, but still… Can you hold me while I hop down? Then I'll sit in the chair again."

"Rio, hopping down steps would jar your injured bones. And there's no need. I had JJ build a ramp. That's where I was while you weren't minding me about not getting out of bed by yourself. I was tugging the ramp into place." She unlocked the wheels and pushed Rio's chair out onto the wide, shaded porch.

Tag ran back and forth between the wheelchair and the ramp, all the while whimpering and uttering short, nervous barks.

"Come here, Tag." Rio snapped his fingers and the Labradoodle scooted toward him. "We have to trust Binney," he declared with confidence as he rubbed Tag's ears. "Both of us," he added, although he wasn't able to glance back and show his appreciation to the woman now edging him onto the ramp. "Binney, forgive me. I knew when I tried to get out of bed alone that it was risky. You're right to be mad at me."

"I'm not mad." She stopped and knelt to be sure his slippered feet were solidly on the footrests. Rising, she began moving him again. "You worried me, though. I'd be hard-pressed to pick you up off the floor if, say, JJ wasn't on the premises?"

"Yeah." Rio sounded repentant. "I haven't thanked you nearly often enough for all of the extra stuff you do. Like the ranch books, typing thank-you notes for the folks who donated to me, playing tunes in the evening on your guitar to help me relax. And now for this wheelchair and ramp. That's… I can't even find the words."

Done negotiating the incline, Binney aimed the chair with hard rubber tires toward the lane. "Honestly, Rio, the variety offered by home care is what I like most about private duty nursing. Speaking of variety, I noticed you have flower beds on each side of the porch steps that need weeding. If it's okay, one of these days when you're napping, I'd like to clean the beds and show off your lovely marigolds."

"My mom planted the flowers. Last time they visited, she nagged me about the weeds. But don't feel you have to pull them. I didn't see weeding listed in your contract."

She laughed, ruffled his hair then swerved around a pothole. "It falls under other duties that may crop up. I gardened some at the Fosters'. I like digging in the dirt."

"Knock yourself out, then. Hey, I see JJ at the small corral. He must not have taken Contessa to the barn. Do you think we can leave the road and go to the corral? The dirt may be rougher, though."

Tag, who trotted close enough to the chair that Rio could keep a hand on him, barked wildly and tore after a rabbit hopping across the road.

Binney called to the dog. "Get back here and leave that poor rabbit alone."

Rio chuckled. "He's always after rabbits and squirrels. As far as I know he never catches them. Do you, boy?" he asked as his pet slunk back acting guilty.

JJ apparently noticed them. He cupped his hands around his mouth and yelled, "Do you need help?" He jogged toward them. When he got closer, he said, "I can move the mare to the barn if it's easier for you to wheel Rio there. The horse was cooped up in the trailer on the drive from Pecos, so I figured she'd like to stretch her legs."

Binney shook her head. "We're doing fine, aren't we, Rio? I should've thought to ask if you were getting bounced around too much."

"I'm great. The only thing that would be better

is if I could get outside under my own power and go back to riding."

"That won't be for a while." Binney squeezed his shoulder. "I hope bringing you out here isn't depressing. We discussed how long it'll take you to heal."

"Don't you go in for another X-ray soon?" JJ asked.

"Next week. I hope the doc says I can lose the hand cast and clavicle brace. It's the most restrictive. I'm sure he'll find my ankle has improved. I can't wait to toss these slippers out and get back to wearing my boots so I'll feel like a cowboy again."

When the men's conversation lagged, Binney said, "Oh, look. Your new mare is coming to the fence to greet you, Rio. She's beautiful. I've only ever seen palominos in old Western movies. How did you happen to decide to raise them? Don't most area breeders raise quarter horses?"

She wheeled Rio right up to the fence. The broadbellied horse stood in grass and watched Tag, who flopped down, panting in a patch of sunlight.

"I have apples in a pack," Binney said. "JJ suggested I bring some." She leaned down and pulled a few from a basket under the seat of the wheelchair.

Rio took one. "JJ, help me walk to the fence."

The ranch manager, used to taking orders from Rio, slanted Binney a questioning glance.

"This ground is fairly level," she said, setting the brake. "I've got the chair as close to the corral as it'll go. So if you feel weak, Rio, you can sit again quickly."

Without his crutch he needed both JJ and Binney's support to walk over the lumpy ground. Still, he leaned on the top rail, fed the mare an apple and rubbed her narrow nose. "You asked why I raise palominos," he remarked. "From known history they're the chosen horses of kings and queens. By the way, palomino is a color, not a true breed. So they may be registered in one of several associations. We follow guidelines set up by the American Saddlebred Horse Association. Palominos generally have calm dispositions. They're good show horses. We've sold a lot to women and girls who do bareback riding or belong to groups who ride in parades." Rio fed the mare a second apple Binney passed him, then he asked to sit down.

She eased him into the chair, but he didn't let go of her, instead he stroked her arms.

Rio's ranch manager cleared his throat. "Rio likes the challenge of raising a genetically perfect palomino herd. Not all horses with palomino characteristics are true palomino. Some are cremellos. They have more of the champagne gene. Some with darker coats are called chocolate palominos. The true color has brown eyes, not blue. Cremellos often have blue eyes."

"All that's interesting," Binney said, slow to disengage herself, but fussing again over Rio, making sure he sat solidly in the chair. "I don't know a lot about horses, but yours are definitely pretty." She stretched out a hand to pet the mare. "When will she have her foal?"

"Late October," the men said in unison.

"Do you think I'll be fit as a fiddle by then?" Rio asked, catching Binney's eye.

She shrugged. "You'll know more after the X-rays. Which reminds me. JJ, I'll need to drive him into the hospital lab in his pickup. Is it gassed up?"

"I'll check. Are you guys going up to the barn?"

She deferred to Rio.

"I'm proud of our setup. I'd like you to see it. The rest of the herd will be grazing in the big field behind the barn. That's a sight. And I should go over some things with JJ in my office."

Nodding, JJ strode off ahead of them.

Enjoying seeing Rio happier than he'd ever appeared, Binney leisurely picked a smooth path to the barn.

Tag hitched himself a ride on Rio's lap.

"I swear that dog is smiling," Binney remarked.

"For an animal that a few years ago didn't trust any human, he now loves being attached to people he trusts."

"Poor thing. He hasn't had many opportunities to sit that close to his most favorite human—you— since we can't let him on your hospital bed, or in your lap when you're taking the TENS treatments."

"Lucky dog's been sleeping with you, though." Rio looped his unfettered arm around Tag, who turned his head and happily licked Rio's face, making the man sputter.

Not knowing whether to laugh at his comment or

take Rio seriously, Binney let his remark slide. "If Tag gets too heavy say so and he'll have to walk."

"Actually he keeps my back pressed to the chair so I sit straighter. That's good because we're traveling over rough terrain."

Binney stopped. "I'm trying to go slow. Is this outing hurting you?" she asked anxiously.

"No. No. I'm happier than a pig in slop to get out of the house. It's not enough to thank you. You deserve way more. Probably candy or flowers—things women covet."

Binney couldn't tell him that his earlier, off-the-cuff *I love you* and even the brotherly kiss on her head would stay with her far longer than any words of thanks he might offer. What she said was: "My job is to get you well."

They'd reached the barn, and JJ, who waited for them there, slid open the big entry door. "Rio's pickup gas tank is nearly full."

"Great. I'm not sure how long he'll be at the hospital clinic. Are you able to keep Tag while we're gone, JJ?"

"Sure thing." He knelt and scrubbed the dog's furry head. "I'll be planting winter grass all week, but he likes to ride on the tractor."

"I should be helping with that," Rio said, sounding glum again.

Binney touched his cheek. "None of that. Your only duty is to take it easy until you heal. What did you want me to see in the barn?"

"The stalls, the tack room, the office. Is the main herd out back?" he asked JJ.

Bobbing his head, the other man moved aside and gestured for Binney to wheel Rio on in.

"Yep, it's a barn," she said, laughing. "Cleaner than most I've seen. But remember for the past year I've done nursing jobs at cattle ranches."

"Since you brought Rio out here, and as barns are old hat to you," JJ said, "I need him to sign Contessa's registry transfer." He pointed to a side door. "Binney, you can take a gander at the rest of our stock. I promise I won't wear Rio out."

She glanced at her watch. "I planned for his first outing to be no more than an hour. I'll give you fifteen minutes. And I'll take Tag." She tugged on the dog's collar. He obediently hopped down from Rio's lap. As they moved away she heard the men talking about seed and fertilizer. It all seemed so natural to her.

Out back the view opened up on a truly beautiful vista. Flat grassy fields were dotted with frolicking golden horses ranging from youngsters to adults. And beyond fenced pastures stretched an array of rolling hills graced with lacy cottonwood and elm trees along with unidentifiable low-growing bushes.

Binney couldn't ever recall being so taken by scenery. It was easy to see why Rio loved the Lonesome Road. Years of hard work to clear so much land and make it habitable probably led to his folks wanting to retire elsewhere. She wondered, though, about a comment Rio had made indicating Ryder's dislike of the ranch. How could identical twins hold such opposing views of the great place where they grew up?

She had fostered in homes of ranch couples so she was aware of the extent of backbreaking labor and deep dedication it took to run a successful ranch. Until being here she'd favored living in town, where there were book and music festivals, and a yearly art walk, to say nothing of restaurants and stores. Now she actually thought she could happily live out here. That had her picturing living here with Rio after he got well, and warmth shot up her body.

Stepping up on the lowest fence rung, she petted a young, curious horse that trotted up shaking a nearly white mane and tail. "Sorry I don't have an apple for you, my beauty," she crooned.

JJ shouted her name, breaking her reverie.

"Are you stuck up there?" he asked from the doorway. "I called you three times. Rio and I are finished, and he's beginning to fade, I think. Although he'll never admit it, so don't tell him I mentioned it."

Binney hopped off the rail. "I'm not stuck. I was woolgathering. Hard not to this place is so gorgeous. Is that your cottage I see tucked into the draw beyond the cultivated land?"

"Yes. Wow, listen to you using terms like draw and cultivated land. Rhonda and I pegged you for a city gal. Although maybe we shouldn't have been so quick to judge after you rode out here on a Harley."

She stuck her two little fingers against her teeth and whistled Tag back from where he'd gone sniffing under a creosote bush. "I read a lot," she said as she and the dog hurried past him.

Grasping the handles of Rio's wheelchair, she murmured, "Sorry I didn't keep track of time. I'll blame it on the lovely tranquility of your ranch." That was better than confessing she'd been daydreaming about him.

"I'm going out to bring in the mare," JJ announced. He settled a brown cowboy hat on his head, exited the barn behind them and closed the door.

It wasn't until after Tag jumped up on his lap again that Rio revisited her comment. "Tranquility is a nice word to describe the Lonesome Road. I've always said this is the only place I can relax and be me."

"JJ seems at home here, too."

"He worked for Dad. JJ and Rhonda dated three or four years before they got engaged and she moved out here part-time. All I hear from most folks is how remote we are. I can't tell you how pleased I am that you get some of what I feel. I don't live in the sticks," he said defiantly.

"Definitely not. It's a charming, unspoiled slice of nature."

They'd almost reached the ramp when Rio said, "Traci Walker called it the sticks when she visited me in the hospital. That's Ryder's term for the ranch, too."

Binney almost lost her grip on the chair. Traci Walker had been the meanest of the mean girls in high school. At least she no longer had to puzzle over Suzette Ferris's oblique comment about one of Rio's hospital visitors. "Is, uh, Traci your girlfriend?"

"Geez, no! We have dated. I gather her dad thinks we still should. But she's way too high-maintenance for me. Do you remember her from high school?"

"Uh, yes."

They were in the house before Rio reached back, caught Binney's hand and tugged her around to where he could see her. "There was a world of angst behind that yes. I remember now you said Ryder stood you up for Traci's sister. According to Traci my brother opted out of going out with them on her recent trip to see Samantha in New York. Probably a first, but from my perspective the Walker girls were raised as queen bees. As a result they both possess a death sting. I hope you know you're ten times the woman, Binney."

"Thanks." Her voice quivered. "Listen, do you need to use the bathroom before we get you back into bed?"

"Yeah. Wheel me to the door and wait while I use the facilities. I loved the outing, but suddenly I'm beat."

"Fresh air can do that." She delivered him to the door, lifted Tag off his lap then assisted him through their routine with practiced ease. But the camaraderie between them had definitely cooled.

Settled in his bed a short time later, Rio yawned. "I'm really sorry I mentioned Traci. She called the other day when you were out after the mail. She thinks I should be healed enough to go to the charity ball at the country club October 1. In case she phones again and you hear us talking, I want you to know I wouldn't go with her if I was well."

"I'm glad you and Ryder both see through her." She smiled down at him, but thought he appeared unhappy. Possibly Rio liked Traci more than he let on. She had visited him in the hospital, after all. And she'd phoned, too, which was more than his brother had done.

"I'm going to feed Tag then go after the mail. I'll fix supper later." Getting no response, she checked back and noted that Rio had fallen asleep.

ALL WEEKEND RIO was extremely nice to her. He held her hand as she read to him during his TENS treatments. He tucked her under his good arm every time she got him up to walk. And he paid her compliments over her guitar playing and other things to the point she was embarrassed.

"Tomorrow are my follow-up X-rays," he said right after Binney finished rubbing in his aftershower lotion. "How about a bedtime good-luck kiss?" He clung to her hand when she went to adjust the head of his bed for sleeping.

She laughed, but leaned down and brushed a kiss over his forehead.

He latched on to the back of her neck with his unbound hand and tugged until their lips met. His mouth teased at first, then hardened into something more serious.

She flattened her palms on his chest, and returned the pressure until he coughed and had difficulty catching his breath. Straightening quickly, she fussed with his pillow. "We got too carried away. Are you all right?"

"I'm fine. Listen, if Doc gets rid of most of these troublesome bandages, and if he says I can start taking care of myself, I still want us to keep seeing each other."

"You don't mean…date?"

"I do. I want you to stay in my life, Binney."

"I'd like that, Rio. A lot." She ran a finger lightly over his lips. Anticipation of joy like none she'd ever experienced flowed through her as she eased away. That night she couldn't sleep. She curled around Tag, but pictured a time when Rio would lie between them.

RETURNING TO THE ranch after Rio's appointment the next day, Binney watched him slump silently in the passenger seat. The visit hadn't gone as he'd hoped. His vertebra showed some improvement, warranting a less chunky collar. But his clavicle hadn't formed enough callus. A nurse cut the cast off his wrist and massaged his hand. She said Dr. Darnell wanted Binney to carry out daily PT for at least two more weeks. And Rio needed to continue using crutches and have help walking until his next visit for a follow-up set of X-rays.

Her attention on the road, Binney tucked her bottom lip between her teeth. "You have made progress, Rio." She tried to return to the closeness they'd shared over the weekend.

He stared ahead, letting his chin rest on the smaller neck collar.

"I know you'd hoped you would no longer need my services. Dr. Darnell said you probably only require my assistance for three more weeks. That's not long."

"Maybe not for you. My life's still stuck in limbo. Can we not talk about this anymore? I'm exhausted after all that poking and prodding."

Worried that she didn't know what more to say to help him, Binney pulled up next to the house.

JJ met them with the wheelchair and an excited Tag. "I wasn't sure he'd still need this chair."

Shooting him a warning scowl, Binney pressed a forefinger to her lips and jerked her head toward where Rio still sat, stone-faced.

"Gotcha," JJ murmured, going around to the passenger door, where he assisted Binney in boosting Rio down. It took both of them to get him into the house and lying flat in the rented hospital bed he'd told JJ that morning they could probably return.

"You two can go," Rio grated, his voice husky with pain Binney judged was emotional.

"I'll stay until he falls asleep," she whispered to JJ. "Dr. Darnell ordered an opiate because of the jarring ride in the pickup. Once I know he's zonked, I think I'll go out and tackle weeding those flower beds by the front porch. I need to do something physical." She continued to speak softly as she trailed

Rio's friend to the door. After closing it behind him, she fed Tag and got out Rio's pill.

"I don't want the damned medicine," Rio insisted, tightening his lips when Binney brought the pill and a glass of water.

"Doctor's orders. You're tense. Take this and unwind. We'll talk about a schedule for your hand therapy after you have a nap."

Tagalong emerged from the kitchen, whined and paced back and forth near the bed.

"Rio, you're even upsetting your dog."

At that he opened his mouth and took the pill.

He was sawing logs by the time she came back from taking the glass to the kitchen. Tag, too, had settled his chin on his paws and he snored softly.

She sighed, but decided to prepare a casserole for dinner.

Because Rio hadn't stirred by the time she finished, she dug out garden gloves she'd had Rhonda buy, left the front door ajar and set out to pull weeds.

In half an hour she'd unearthed two rosebushes and rows of marigolds. Hearing a vehicle traveling the ranch road, she sat back on her heels, assuming it was Rhonda. But looking around she was surprised to see a dark blue car instead. In her time at the ranch, no one had come to visit Rio. *Oh, boy, she hoped it wasn't Traci Walker.*

The car braked a foot from where Binney knelt. Dust rolled over her. She sputtered and got to her feet as the vehicle made a sweeping turn heading out toward the highway again. Probably someone was lost.

She shed her gloves and dropped them in the bucket of weeds as a well-dressed woman perhaps a few years older than her emerged from the still-running car.

"Is this where Rio McNabb lives?"

"It is, but he's sleeping. He was injured at a rodeo several weeks ago." Binney walked toward the woman. But the driver hurried around to the passenger side, where she opened the door and removed a wicker basket and two large totes.

Curious, Binney figured someone had belatedly sent Rio get-well gifts. However, she was rendered mute when the woman plopped both totes at her feet and shoved the bulky wicker basket so solidly into her midsection that Binney nearly lost her breath.

"That's Rio McNabb's son," the woman stated in a no-nonsense voice. "He's a month old. My sister birthed him at home with a midwife. Something went horribly, horribly wrong." Her voice cracked as she tottered around the front of the car on spiky heels and paused again by the open driver's door and started to get in.

"Wait!" Binney couldn't take a step as the totes hemmed her in.

"Lindsey bled to death on the way to the hospital or she would have contacted the baby's father. I'm sure she would've wanted me to keep Rex Quintin, but I work erratic shifts at a busy casino on the Vegas Strip. The same one where Lindsey dealt blackjack. Had she lived, we'd have raised her kid, but…" The woman's voice gave out and she dashed at tears. "I had to dig to find McNabb, the scum. If you're the little woman he leaves behind when he rodeos and paints a town red, I'm sorry. I can see you're shocked. I warned Lindsey time and again not to trust foot-loose cowboys, but she fell hard for the jerk." After piling into the car, the woman slammed her door, gunned the engine and sped toward the highway, leaving a rooster tail of dust and much more in her wake.

The dust had settled around her before Binney recovered enough to peek inside the basket, where a baby slept.

Chapter Seven

Waves of shock washed through Binney, welding her boots to a spot next to Rio's porch steps even after the blue car had disappeared from sight. Its dust had totally dissipated by the time she quit reeling enough to chastise herself for not committing to memory the number on the license plate. *It had been a Nevada plate, all right.*

But as her initial stunned feelings subsided, stilling her racing heart, a realization of the impact of what had just transpired kick-started her still-addled brain. Not only had she failed to mentally log the license number, she hadn't asked the woman's name, nor inquired about the last name of the baby's birth mother.

Other emotions coursed through her one after another. Disappointment in Rio. Not just because he'd kissed her and had said he wanted her to remain in his life when he had had another relationship on a not-so-back burner, although that stung her personally. She felt sorrow for the baby, who, like her, would grow up without a mother.

Suddenly cold in spite of standing in the late-summer sunshine, Binney shivered and wished she could hop on her Harley and leave this job right now. She had again let her heart get too invested in a McNabb twin.

Of course she couldn't run off. She had to take Rio his son, and continue doing her job until he was able to make other arrangements.

After what seemed like an eternity of fence-straddling passed, she tamped down the ache in the back of her throat. Telling herself Rio's problems didn't truly matter, she juggled the basket and the two totes and went into the house.

Rio was apparently just waking up. His eyelids fluttered, but sprung wide when Binney kicked the door closed with a loud bang.

Smothering a yawn, he cleared his throat. "How long have I been sawing logs? We missed lunch. I'm starved." Finally noticing that she was laboring under a burden, he blinked a few more times. "What's all that? Did Rhonda go shopping? If so, why isn't she or JJ helping you carry stuff in?"

Binney dropped the totes at the foot of his bed, pressed the button to raise his torso to a partial incline and set the wicker basket across his thighs.

"What's this?" He grasped one of the handles with his newly freed hand, but because it still lacked full mobility he wasn't able to bend down the side to see in the basket.

Tag, who'd also been sleeping below the bed, woke up and shook himself hard. He whined and leaped up until both feet rested on the bed. Snuffling the basket, he proceeded to bark. And he barked until the occupant of the basket awakened and began to cry.

Rio let go of the basket rim and reared back as if he'd been burned. "Binney...what the hell?"

Urging the dog away from the bed, she ordered him to sit. Fixing Rio with her sternest nurse's glare, she unloaded on him. "Well, Rio, this is your son. He didn't come by stork, but did arrive special delivery. The woman who brought him claimed she's his aunt. He's a month old." Her voice faltered. "I'm sorry to be the one to tell you his mom unfortunately is deceased." Her throat worked and her voice gave out.

As much as Binney wanted to watch Rio squirm, she couldn't bear to let the baby sob. She scooped him out of his makeshift bassinet, held him to her shoulder, swayed and crooned to him until his crying lessened.

"What in the devil are you talking about? Whose kid is it, really?"

"Rio, the woman who drove in and left you this bundle of joy said her sister gave birth to your baby at home. I'm so sorry, but something went wrong and she di...died on the way to the hospital. In Las Vegas. Her first name was Lindsey. The sister said you two met at a rodeo. Were you in Nevada at a rodeo about ten months ago?"

"I've ridden in a lot of Vegas rodeos. But I swear I did not father this baby or any other. Why would you take the kid and let some crazy woman leave without first talking to me?"

"Don't you go blaming me, Rio McNabb. I had no choice. I was weeding. She drove in and turned her car around. It blew dust all over me. I thought she had gotten lost, but she pulled these bags and the basket out of her car and shoved them on me with very little explanation. Before I could catch my breath she drove off like a bat out of hell."

"Well, she lied. Get her back."

"How? She conveniently didn't share her sister's last name, or say who she was." Binney jiggled the baby. "I think he's wet. Or hungry. I need to see if she left anything to solve either of those problems. Can you hold him a minute? Crook your good arm, please."

"Oh, I don't know…" He did follow her edict, but with a sour face.

She moved the basket, setting it aside after placing the crying baby in the curve of Rio's arm. The infant instantly stopped crying and gazed up at the man holding him with huge dark blue eyes.

Seeing the two engrossed in staring at each other made Binney smile. Then Rio looked up and scowled at her, and she quickly dived into the totes. "Ah, diapers, wet wipes and premixed formula. Oh, what have we here? A packet of papers." She pulled them out.

"The top one lists his feeding and sleeping schedules. That's helpful." She flipped to the next page. "There's a certificate from the midwife about his

birth. It verifies he was born at home in the state
of Nevada."

"What does it say? Does it give the mother's full
name?" Rio demanded while trying to peer down
over the cervical collar once the baby he held began
to suck on one of his own chubby hands. The respite
didn't last long and was followed by louder cries,
from which Rio recoiled.

Binney set the papers aside. "First things first.
Let's see to it that he's dry and fed. A cursory glance
at his schedule shows he's past due for a bottle."

"Dammit, Binney. We have to find out where he
really belongs."

Digging into the bag again, she found a puddle
pad, which she laid on Rio's lap. Taking the baby,
she unsnapped the short rompers he wore, removed
the soaked diaper and, while holding the baby's feet,
she folded the sticky edges together. Scooting Tagalong away with her toe, she set the wet item on the
tile floor between her feet. Deftly she opened a dry
diaper and in seconds had restored it along with his
rompers. "Here, hold him again," she said, passing
the now gurgling infant to Rio. "I need to find a
plastic bag for dirty diapers, dispose of this one and
wash my hands before I warm a bottle."

"How did you do that?"

"Do what?" she asked, gazing back over her
shoulder.

"You changed that diaper so efficiently."

"Yes, I'm a trained nurse," she said, setting out
for the kitchen.

"I thought you only took care of old ranchers," Rio called.

"Nurses work with patients of all ages," Binney yelled back. "And I update my skills with professional development courses every so often."

She took care of what needed doing. On returning to the living room, she noticed the baby had grabbed on to one of Rio's fingers. "Hey, cowboy, you sort of have the magic touch yourself. That's good, because I need to put his bottle in warm water for a few minutes."

Rio wasted no time shaking his finger loose. He glowered at Binney. "Take him with you. By the way, does the kid have a name?"

"The aunt called him Rex Quintin."

"Maybe Quintin is really his last name. I don't know anyone around here by that name, but she obviously left him at the wrong ranch."

Binney leveled a look of sympathy, but shook her head. "She began by asking for you by name, Rio." She grabbed one of the baby's bottles. "Let me take care of readying his bottle then I'll see if I can remember everything she said, which wasn't much. She rocked me back on my heels with her news, too." Clenching the bottle, Binney dashed back to the kitchen. Her legs were still unsteady, and her stomach was one icy pit.

It wasn't long before she returned to take the baby. She sat in one of the recliners, and watched as the infant latched on to the bottle's nipple and sucked greedily.

Binney had draped a clean receiving blanket over her shoulder. Every so often she raised baby Rex up, rubbed his back and waited for him to burp, which he did with gusto.

The second time, Rio said, "What's in that bottle? Beans? The kid burps like a cowboy at a roundup."

"He was hungry and drank too fast. If he didn't burp, gas would build in his tummy. He'd be uncomfortable and cry. Babies cry if they're wet, hungry or gassy."

"Thanks. I can't see why I need to know that. We've gotta find the woman who dropped him off and give him back ASAP."

Binney heard Rio's stomach rumble. "When Rex finishes his bottle I'll go put a tuna casserole I assembled earlier in the oven. We can have it with more of the bread I made into French toast this morning."

"I know I said I was starved, but why are you deliberately dragging your feet about checking the paper you said verified his birth?"

"I'm not deliberately dragging my feet, Rio. A wet, hungry baby in the house takes precedence over adult wants."

"That's my point. A wet, hungry baby does not belong in my house."

His words hit Binney like a punch to her stomach that she couldn't prevent from cramping and churning. She brushed kisses over baby Rex's fuzzy head. Sympathy welled for a poor baby that no one seemed to want. Was that how she'd come to be left on the agency doorstep?

"Why are you staring at me like I'm a horrible person?" Rio asked harshly.

"Perhaps because you took in a stray dog, but seem only too ready to kick an innocent baby to the curb."

Rio retreated into a shell. Rex slurped the last of the milk from his bottle. Climbing to her feet, Binney set the bottle on the coffee table. The baby settled his face into the side of her neck as she marched to Rio's bed and snatched up the papers she'd stuffed back into the tote earlier. Shaking a page in front of his nose she said, "This is a certificate stating the baby was born at home in the city of Las Vegas." She read off a date and time. "It's verified by a midwife. The baby's name is Rex Quintin McNabb."

She held it steady so he could see it. "Lindsey Ann Cooper, age twenty-five, is shown as the birth mother. The aunt said she would have contacted you if she hadn't died."

Taking the fluttering paper in his own shaking hand, Rio hauled in a deep breath. "I'm telling you I don't know any Lindsey Ann Cooper. If the rodeo was in town she must've pulled my name off one of the flyers. They're distributed everywhere."

Binney spun the rocking chair around and plopped down. "The sister said she works in a busy casino on the Vegas Strip where her sister dealt blackjack. The aunt called you scum, a jerk and, further, said she'd warned her sister to stay away from footloose cowboys. Think hard, Rio. Were you drinking in a casino, maybe after winning some big event? Although the aunt sounded as if it was more than a one-night stand. But then she ranted on about you painting the town red and leaving me behind, because I guess she assumed I was your wife, so I don't know."

Shutting his eyes, Rio plainly tried to curb his mounting irritation by rubbing his temples repeatedly. "I'm telling you, since I decided to buy the ranch six years ago, all winnings not needed for entry fees and travel went to my dad and to buy horses. Gambling was never my thing, and I don't drink except for a rare beer with buddies after a significant win. I park my pickup and camper on the rodeo grounds so I don't have to pay for a hotel. I can't remember the last time I walked through a casino." He finished speaking and silence filled the living room.

Binney got awkwardly to her feet. "I'm going to put the casserole in the oven."

Tag clambered up as if knowing she'd feed him, too.

Rio picked up his phone. "I hope you have enough for JJ. I want him to come over and talk about this issue since you're sure not on my side."

The chill taking root in Binney expanded. She rubbed the baby's back and turned away, recalling how in high school the twins and many in their privileged crowd skipped out of taking responsibility for even slight indiscretions. Recently she'd started believing that Rio had changed—had grown up. "Rio, for the life of me I can't see why a pregnant woman would lie about her baby's father or pick a total stranger to pin it on. Especially since the poor woman's sister insinuated if her sister had lived they wouldn't have needed you. On the other hand you seem so adamantly opposed."

"I am!" He practically stared a hole through her, then glanced down and punched a number on his cell phone.

Binney left the living room. As she waited for the oven to heat up enough to stick in the casserole, she fed Tag and worried over baby Rex's fate.

She got out plates and silverware using one hand. Since they were having a supper guest she should probably add a salad to their skimpy meal. That required doing something with Rex. While deciding she'd have to prevail on Rio to hold him, she heard the front door open. Maybe she ought to let the men talk by themselves. But she also wanted to listen to their exchange.

"What's all this?" JJ asked. He locked eyes with Binney as she came into the room with the baby in spite of Tagalong bounding between them and playfully butting his head against JJ's knee.

Rio answered from his bed. "Ha! That's almost the exact question I asked. Brace yourself for Binney's tall tale, buddy."

"You tell it, then," she snapped at Rio. "I need to fix a salad to go with supper. Without a front pack, or someplace secure to lay Rex, you'll have to supply your arm again."

Rio balked as if he'd object, but didn't, and made space in the crook of his arm.

"Is that a real live kid?" JJ moved closer. "Cute. But what's a baby doing here?"

After making sure Rio had a good hold on the baby, Binney stepped away from his bed.

"You tell him the story before you go," Rio pleaded. "It's so damned preposterous I'm sure to get something wrong."

Binney pinched the bridge of her nose. "I was out weeding the flower beds."

JJ nodded. "You did a good job. They look nice. Linda's going to love them."

"Who?"

"Rio's mom. Rob and I took care of the cattle, barn and fields. Linda handled the house, garden and flowers before Rio bought the ranch."

"Your dad's name is Rob?" Binney asked Rio. "I guess that makes all the male McNabb names start with the letter *R*."

Rio's brows dived together. "Just tell the damned story."

Binney set her hands on her hips. "Okay. In the middle of my weeding a car drove in and stopped." Gesturing this time, she repeated verbatim the story she'd given Rio.

JJ's mouth fell open. He rubbed the back of his neck and gaped at Rio after Binney fell silent. "You're positive you never met Ms. Cooper?"

"Never!" Rio said harshly. "And because we don't know the name of the woman who dropped the kid here, I think we need to call Abilene's social services and have someone come get him." He reached for his phone.

Binney gasped and the men both reacted with a start. "They won't take him, Rio," she said. "Like it or not, the midwife put your name down as the baby's father. Do you want to be investigated for possible child abandonment?"

JJ broke into the middle of their dagger-tossing match. "She has a point. I know you were at a clinic today, but you need to call and get an appointment for a DNA test."

"I should have thought of that," Binney exclaimed.

Waving his little arms around, the baby started to fuss again.

Tag left JJ's side and trotted over to the bed. Propping his feet on the side rail, he sniffed the baby through the bars.

Rio lifted his arm. "Tag, stop deviling the poor little guy."

JJ scanned the room. "Is this all the woman brought? If you can't return the kid ASAP to the aunt you need some baby furniture and stuff."

Binney picked Rex up, pulled a bottle of water out of one tote and sat in the rocker, offering him a drink.

Tagalong left the bed to set his chin on Binney's knee. It was clear he didn't know what to make of the baby. She let him sniff Rex, which satisfied the dog.

Rio sat eyeing the domestic scene. "I'd go now if I thought the lab was open after five o'clock. I want this settled. Since I have to wait until morning to call, what do you recommend I do in the meantime?"

"You can't do a lot, Rio. I'll take care of him," Binney promised.

"Where will he sleep? Like JJ said, the woman who dumped him off only provided bare essentials."

"True. I cannot believe she drove all the way from Vegas with a baby in a wicker basket. What if she'd been in a wreck?"

JJ sat beside Binney. "You said you have to make a salad. Give him to me. I need practice. Rhonda and I are going to get married soon and we want to start a family."

"You can't get married until I'm a hundred percent," Rio said. "I know Rhonda is planning a big church shindig. I'm not going to be your best man on crutches and wearing this stupid neck collar with my tuxedo."

"You'll be recovered. Rhonda's lifelong dream is having a Christmas wedding. If it was up to me," he said, accepting the baby Binney handed him, "I'd go down to the courthouse and find a justice of the peace. You gals put big emphasis on all the wedding folderol."

"Not me." Binney gave JJ the bottle.

"Why not you?" The question came from Rio.

She stopped at the kitchen doorway. "I don't know. I guess because all of my energies were focused on becoming an RN and then work." She went on into the kitchen, but now her mind seemed stuck on wondering, if most women had long-standing wedding wishes, what was wrong with her? She'd been in nursing friends' weddings and had been happy for them. Really, she'd never spared time to date much even though some interns had hit on her. Her best friends in nursing swore med students and interns were only hunting for a meal ticket until they became docs and made money, then they frequently divorced. She had witnessed the truth to that.

What few thoughts she'd had on wedding folde-rol, as JJ called the white dress and trappings, took a backseat to her lifelong dream of wanting to belong in a family. She'd dwelled on stepping into a ready-made one with grandparents, parents and siblings. She hadn't envisioned a husband. *How silly was that?*

Brushing aside the images, she tossed a salad. Seeing the casserole was almost ready to be served, she stuck her head in the living room. "Do you guys want me to bring plates to you on trays, or shall I set the table in here? Rio, you traveled to town today, do you feel like sitting in a kitchen chair?"

"I'm okay. JJ and I were just discussing all of us driving in to the big box store after supper to pick up a cradle or crib, that front pack you mentioned and anything else you think we'll need for the little dude until I get his true paternity straightened out. JJ said he thinks DNA tests may take as much as two weeks to get results."

"Maybe. Not my area of expertise." She crossed the room and took Rex from JJ. The baby was wide awake and happily blowing bubbles from his rose-bud mouth.

She didn't have to ask JJ to help Rio from his bed.

He just did it. And Rio appeared steadier on his feet, moving toward the kitchen on his crutches.

They all sat around the kitchen table, and she and JJ passed Rex back and forth while she dished out food. Then she took the baby back and held him in her left arm, preparing to eat with her right hand until she noticed Rio frowning. "What's wrong? I'm not going to drop hot tuna and noodles on him. Haven't you seen moms do this in restaurants?"

"Mostly their little ones are strapped into high chairs. We'll buy one of those."

JJ stopped shoveling casserole into his mouth and wiped his lips with a napkin. "Are you sure you want to buy a lot of baby stuff, Rio? You say he's not yours. With his mother gone, and his aunt not assuming responsibility, you're eventually going to have to turn him over to local child services. Why get left with a bunch of baby furnishings?"

Binney sat up straighter. "I wish I was in a position to apply to adopt him. I know an unmarried nurse who did that. But she works set hospital shifts. Maybe I could find a sitter and go back to the hospital," she mused. Tightening her arm around the bundle, she gazed lovingly down on the infant.

Both men fixed her with disbelieving stares. Rio broke the tense silence. "I know you have a big heart, and I can see you care, but you love home nursing."

"I do, but…"

JJ stated the obvious. "You don't own a car. I doubt any children's court would approve of you hauling a baby to a sitter's on a Harley."

Thrusting out a defiant chin, she gestured with her fork. "I can buy a car."

"Why would you?" Rio asked huffily. "You don't have any connection to his family, whoever they are."

Tears filled her eyes and spilled over. "I know what it's like to grow up a throwaway child. One committed parent is better than living among a raft of people who don't care one iota if you live or die."

"Didn't you live with foster families?" JJ asked. "I didn't figure that would be much different than having regular folks."

"Believe me, it is in some cases. If you aren't cute and sweet enough to be adopted, you may get treated more like an indentured servant. If the family has birth kids and they don't like you, everything that goes wrong is your fault. And I can attest that it's no picnic living in a group home. By then most unwanted teens are cranky and mad at the world. And city cops shake them down at the first sign of trouble."

"Have you ever tried to find your parents?" Rio asked quietly. "Like, I'm wondering how hard it'd be to find the woman who dumped Rex off here."

"I have no desire to find the people who abandoned me. You never met Rex's aunt. She didn't know me from Adam and yet was willing to plop him in my hands. She couldn't make tracks out of here fast enough. I don't want to find her. He needs someone to raise him who cares," she said fiercely.

"This conversation is pointless," JJ said. "If we're

going to drive to the store before it closes, we should finish eating."

Binney was gratified to see Rio looked troubled by the turn of their conversation. What that meant she wasn't sure. Just a few days ago he'd said he wanted her to remain in his life. He'd said nothing about that now. She kept returning to the fact he had admitted to riding in rodeos in Las Vegas. It still made no sense to her that a woman of twenty-five would pluck a strange guy's name off a rodeo flyer—why? Because she had a thing for cowboys and found them interchangeable? If not Rio, who was Rex's father? Was it someone Lindsey wanted to keep hidden from her sister, or perhaps from people where they worked? Had she dallied with a boss? Maybe a married one.

She fell silent and they all tucked into their food, but tension in the room didn't dissipate. Finally, Binney said, "We need to chill. All our arguing has upset Tag. Have you noticed he's pacing around the table? If he senses something's wrong, Rex surely feels it, too."

Rio set down his fork. "Supper was good, Binney. Look, I didn't mean to hit so many of your hot buttons. I'm sorry you had a hard life. You've come a long way all on your own. I just wish we knew Rex's real story is all. He is kinda cute, but little and helpless. I've never been around any babies. This is all unnerving to me."

"I understand that, Rio. I really do. But you can

speak out for yourself. Rex has no one to advocate for him."

"I don't know. I'd say you're doing a pretty good job."

Binney wasn't sure from his tone how Rio meant that. Did he want her to get out of their lives?

Rising, JJ cleared the table and took plates to the sink. "Can we load the dishwasher when we get back from the store?"

"Fine by me." Binney handed him the casserole dish. "Will you put this and the leftover salad in the fridge while I change the baby?"

Rio scooted back his chair. "JJ, will you drive? Your pickup bed is longer than mine. We'll be hauling my wheelchair as well as bringing home whatever we buy."

"Rhonda works late tonight. She won't believe any of this if I try and explain over the phone. Binney, do you mind if I have her meet us at the store so I can fill her in?"

"I don't have any problem. But it's not my story to tell. My name's not on the midwife's record."

"Mine shouldn't be, either," Rio charged. "But, Rhonda's not going to broadcast to the world."

Binney sent him a searing glance. Why did he care what the greater world thought?

JJ came back from the fridge and helped Rio stand. "I'll go bring my pickup down to the house. Binney, can you handle getting Rio and the baby out front?"

"Sister Mary Margaret always told us where

there's a will there's a way. I'll manage. I know you'll drive on back roads so I'll sit in back and hold on to the baby's basket until we get a car seat. That's the most important. I'll make a list of what else we need. Shall we take Tag, or leave him here?"

"Take him. He's family," Rio said, as he hobbled across the kitchen to the bathroom.

His touchy tone gave Binney pause. Just where did that leave Rex? Unfortunately it was as if Rio had drawn a very clear line in the sand. Tagalong was family. This poor child who bore his name wasn't.

Chapter Eight

They didn't buy out the store, but had put a serious dent in the baby aisle. Rio had generously told her and Rhonda to purchase whatever they thought was necessary.

After checking out, Binney installed the safety-rated car seat in the second seat of JJ's king cab. Now, with Rio in the passenger seat, she drove JJ's vehicle back to the ranch. He had opted to ride home with Rhonda.

While at the store they all kept deferring to Binney. Probably because she was a nurse, but also plainly the one most attached to Rex. It did cross her mind that perhaps she shouldn't lavish so much attention on the baby, because her role at the Lonesome Road was as caregiver to Rio, the man who'd hired her.

In streetlights that shone in through the pickup windows, Binney chanced to see how weary Rio appeared. His head was pressed tight against the headrest and his eyes were closed. In the flickering light she could see he had dark smudges underneath his eyes.

"Are you okay?" she asked softly, just loud enough to be heard over Tagalong shuffling around in his portion of the backseat. "You've had a long day. How's the left hand doing? We need to work in the therapy session after we get home."

Rio opened his eyes. "Of necessity a rancher puts in long days. Am I really getting better? I don't hurt, but I feel out of sorts, and I'm beyond done in."

"You started the day thinking the doctor would say you'd almost be back to normal. All that got knocked aside before you were handed a baby and that jarring news. I'm really sorry I let the woman from Nevada get away. I was stunned, to say the least."

"I suppose anyone would have been. It's not every day a person gets a baby handed to them. What all do you need to do before lights out tonight? Anything I can help with?"

"I have to assemble the crib and give Rex his night feeding. Will you want a shower, or can you wait and take one in the morning? Baby or no baby, you're my patient and come first, Rio."

"Yeah. I wish that wasn't true, either. Even more I wish you believed me when I say I don't know anyone named Lindsey Cooper."

Chewing on the inside of her lower cheek, Binney let out a sigh. "I believe you're convinced the woman and her sister made a mistake. I also know you recently hit your head hard enough in that rodeo accident to knock you out. I've seen where an injury like that can cause short- or even long-term amnesia."

His eyes narrowed. "You're saying you think I've lost some of my marbles?"

"Not lost forever. But I saw a video on the news of your accident. You were knocked out and they carried you out of the arena before you came to. Furthermore, you claim you don't remember me from high school, yet I can describe your favorite shirt. Blue with white pearl buttons and an applique of a bucking horse on both breast pockets."

"I think you're making that up."

"I'm not. Come on, you wore it two days out of five your senior year."

Rhonda and JJ passed her at the turnoff to the ranch road.

"I've owned a lot of Western shirts with horse appliques," Rio said after a period devoid of talk. "But there is absolutely no way I'd forget in ten or so months what you're accusing me of forgetting."

She shrugged and stopped next to Rhonda's car. "Have it your way, Rio. Tomorrow we'll go get your and Rex's DNA tested." Setting the emergency brake, she vaulted out of the pickup.

Rhonda scurried to unlock the house. JJ dropped the tailgate and muscled out Rio's wheelchair. Binney unstrapped Rex from his new car seat. Tag ran back and forth overseeing the humans. Soon everything was out of the pickup except for Rio and small packages left in the cab.

JJ gestured to Binney. "Let Rhonda take the baby

and his basket inside while I see to Rio. You can re-move the car seat. You'll need it tomorrow in Rio's pickup."

Rhonda accepted Rex, but hesitated beside Rio's open door. "Now that I've heard the whole story, Rio, it's too ludicrous to not be fiction."

"Binney thinks the crack I took when my head connected with the fence at the rodeo grounds wiped my memory of having sex with a woman in Nevada."

JJ spewed a snort as he helped Rio into the wheel-chair. "Convenient, if that was your MO. I've been around you since you competed in junior rodeos. For you to have gone so far off the rails is completely out of character. And I can't believe a woman you'd have had to know very well would be forgettable, Rio."

Listening, Binney fumbled unhooking the car seat. JJ's casual statement left her heart aching. On day one Rio had established how forgettable she was to him. And they had attended the same schools for several years.

However, maybe she was wrong. In the time she'd been caring for Rio, he didn't seem the type of man who'd make love with a woman then drop her like a hot rock. Just things he said about his folks, about the ranch, about his horses, labeled him a good person.

"I thought you said removing the seat would only take a few minutes?" JJ spoke from directly behind her.

Rising up fast, Binney hit her head on the door frame. She let out a yelp and rubbed the spot she'd smacked against the unforgiving metal.

"You okay?" He paused long enough for her to nod, then said, "Sorry, I thought you heard me walk up. I helped Rio into bed. Rhonda left him with the baby. She went on up to our house. I wonder if you should contact social services for Rio. I keep going back to the fact there's no proof the woman, the aunt who dumped off the kid, didn't catch Rio's accident on the news and figure she'd found a patsy. It's devious, but some people are."

The car seat came loose with a force almost causing Binney to fall. "Really, JJ? Why? She cried in front of me. She drove here from Nevada. And there's the midwife's note stamped with a date commensurate with the baby's age. You suggested DNA tests. Are you changing your mind?"

"No, but something feels fishy to me."

"Your truck is ready, and I've removed the car seat."

He accepted the ignition key, but heaved a sigh. "I feel sorry for Rio."

"Me, too, JJ. But..." Her thought trailed and she trudged on up to the house. She, too, sighed before opening the door. If she put herself in Rio's shoes, she did see how he could be emotionally drained.

It surprised her to see him sitting with the head of his bed elevated to where he could stare at the baby inside the basket on his lap. "I thought you'd be asleep," she said, leaving the car seat near the door.

"At the store, women who passed us went on about how cute the little guy was, and everyone assumed I was his dad. One even said, 'Oh, your daddy is all banged up.' I remember a bronc rider and his wife showing off their new baby at a rodeo. Some guys said the baby resembled his wife, others swore he was the spitting image of Owen, the papa. This fellow has dark curly hair, like mine. Outside of that he looks like a million other babies to me."

Just then Rex opened his eyes and stared up at Rio. His eyes were huge and black or midnight blue. "Look at his eyes, Binney. Mine are gray. Honestly, I'm going crazy making useless parallels. If you bring me a bottle I'll feed the kid while you start putting the crib together. I wish I could do that, but obviously I can't."

"The kid has a name," she snapped in exasperation, but crossed to dig a bottle of premixed formula from one of the totes left by the baby's aunt.

"Yeah. But I know a guy, a rodeo clown, who named his dog Rex. Seems more fitting than sticking a boy with that handle."

She cracked a smile. "Actually Rex is Latin for king. Maybe Lindsey Cooper had lofty ideals for her son and that's why she chose you," she said, softening her tone a lot.

Squalling came from the depths of the basket.

Tag jumped up and trotted up to the bed, whining first at Rio, then Binney. She took the baby out of the basket and put him in Rio's arms then wiggled a new bottle. "I'll go warm this."

"What about the crib assembly?"

"I'll bring back a knife to open the box."

From the kitchen she could hear Rio either trying

to calm the baby or talking to his pet. She thought baby Rex was winning over the not-so-tough cowboy. She returned quickly and opened the crib box, trying not to smile over how the infant had quieted just being held against Rio's muscular chest. She wouldn't mind laying her head there, either.

"I thought you'd decided to buy a full-sized crib," Rio said when she leaned the narrow mattress against one of the recliners.

"I debated between this one and a travel one that was more like a playpen. It cost less, but had a playpen bottom and mesh sides. It would've served him far longer than it'll take to get results from a DNA. Besides, it'll be months before he crawls and needs a playpen."

She noticed Rio staring into space for a few minutes until he focused on the directions she placed in his weaker hand. Wondering what was going through his mind, rather than risk asking and opening another discussion about calling social services, she went after the bottle.

Relieving him of the directions, she put a burp cloth over his arm and settled him with the baby and the bottle. At times she sneaked a peek at him as she assembled the crib. Her feelings remained jumbled with the advent of the baby in their lives. Rex was wonderfully uncomplicated. Grown men, not so much.

"Check this out, Binney. Is he trying to hold his bottle? Is that common?" Rio asked.

She almost said *your son is precocious*. Canceling that comment, she met Rio's steady gaze and chuckled. "He's trying, but he's a little young to have a firm enough grip. It'll be six or seven months before he can be left to drink on his own."

"Last year JJ and I hand-raised a foal the mother refused to nurse. At the time I wondered how a mother who gave birth could turn her back on her baby."

Thinking of her own life, Binney swallowed a lump. "Yeah, it defies reason."

"Damn! Shame on me," he said with genuine regret. "I forgot your circumstances."

"It is what it is." She got up and helped him burp Rex, because plainly it was a struggle for him. His remark did make her feel teary-eyed over a circumstance she hadn't cried about in years.

With the bottle empty, and because she still battled shaky insides, she turned her back on Rio and set the empty bottle on the coffee table. Crossing the room she detached the infant seat from the car seat base and brought it back to place it in the recliner. "I'll change his diaper since you probably can't manage that yet, and put him in sleepers I saw in one of the totes. That way you won't have to hold him on your lap while you direct me in the final crib assembly."

"I can't unsay what I said, Binney. I'd never purposely hurt you."

"I know." Except for the crinkling tote bag and the gurgling baby, the room remained oppressively quiet. Finally as she changed Rex, she said, "I shouldn't be so sensitive over something that happened a lifetime ago. And technically Rex's mom didn't turn her back on him, her sister did that."

Rio said nothing until she went to buckle Rex in his seat. "I know we determined you aren't in any position to adopt him, but you'd be a good mother, Binney."

The sadness merely thinking of Rex being adopted by strangers, or growing up without a real home as she had, weighed heavily on her heart. "Your saying that means a lot to me, Rio," she said, letting their gazes connect and hold.

Time stretched like a rubber band. Tag woofed, and Binney shook off an odd longing that she and Rio could, together, make a perfect family, a perfect home for Rex.

The feeling persisted, not dimming in the least as with Rio's concise directions and her mechanical ability, they got the crib assembled, and even managed to negate the earlier tension with a few self-deprecating laughs along the way.

"I hope I can get this through the door to my bedroom," Binney said, critically eyeing the finished product.

"Why not leave it out here?" Rio asked around a yawn. "I'm a light sleeper, but Tag will also sound an alarm so I can send him to wake you. That way I won't have to lie here listening to the baby cry, and not be in any shape to do anything about it."

"I would never sleep through his crying, but it's your call," she murmured, carefully shifting the sleeping baby into the crib. That settled, she turned out lights, said good-night to Rio and went to her bedroom pondering if any of what just happened meant he had mellowed toward his son. She still thought some kink in his brain following his horrific accident must be causing him to not recall Lindsey Cooper.

Chapter Nine

Awakened around 2:00 a.m. by Rex crying, Binney crawled out of bed to take care of his feeding. She almost tripped over Tag, who came whining at her bedroom door. Sashing a robe around shorty pajamas, she stopped at the kitchen to put a bottle she'd stashed there on to warm then hurried over to calm the baby and change his diaper before Rio shouted for her.

She soon laughed, because in spite of Rio saying he was a light sleeper, he apparently hadn't heard the baby's cries or Tag's signals. After completing the comfort routine with still no movement from Rio's bed, she went over to see that he was all right.

The rise and fall of his broad chest as he lay on his back was easy to identify in moonlight streaming through the patio sliding glass doors. Binney was oh so tempted to smooth back a lock of dark hair that flopped appealingly over his forehead. Her fingers itched to do so.

Reminded of the stress Rio had endured throughout the over-long day, she juggled the baby and resisted touching or waking him. "Your daddy needs his rest," she murmured in the baby's ear on her way to collect his bottle.

As if he understood, Rex waved his arms and gurgled, even blowing a few bubbles that made Binney smile and kiss his soft dark hair. He was so sweet it gave her physical pain to think tests might prove Rio wasn't his dad. He needed one reliable parent. She knew she was falling in love with Rex and Rio. Her head told her that wasn't wise. Her heart didn't listen well.

Tag yawned, but he shadowed her in and out of the kitchen. And when she later took a seat in the rocker, he sniffed the baby then flopped down at her feet. Twice during the feeding, Rio stirred restlessly. But he didn't wake up.

In the still night, while Rex happily sucked down his formula, Binney used the quiet time to plan for the next day. But her mind kept veering off to a dream of the family she and Rio and Rex could be.

RIO SLOWLY WOKE up to sunlight and the smell of frying bacon. He blinked a few times and experienced some new body aches after he pressed the button to raise the head of his bed. He didn't hear Tag shuffling around. And the baby's crib stood empty.

He rattled the side rail trying to slide it down. It didn't budge.

"Binney," he called, loudly since she had to be in the kitchen.

She appeared in the archway at once holding

a spatula. Rio realized she had the baby strapped around her in the front pack they'd bought the night before. For some reason it made him smile.

"Good morning, sleepyhead."

"What time is it?" Rio stifled a yawn. "Did the baby sleep the whole night through?"

"It's six fifteen. He roused Tag and me at two, but you snored through it."

"I do not snore. Do I?"

"Actually, no. But you slept like the dead. Can you give me a minute? I'm putting waffles in the warming oven along with bacon. Decide if you want breakfast first, or a shower."

"I can wait." She disappeared and Rio ran his right hand over his prickly jaw. His stomach growled so it wanted food. But as discombobulated as he felt, he needed a shower and shave to come fully awake.

The next time Binney showed up, he'd won his battle with the side rail and sat dangling his legs over the side of the hospital bed. "Will the food keep if I shower and get rid of my fuzzy face first?"

"No problem." She passed him his crutch and slipped her shoulder beneath his opposite arm. He wobbled a tad so she tightened her hold around his waist. Her fingers had slid under his loose shirt. "Steady there. Rio, are you okay? Did you overdo things yesterday?"

"I'm good." He brushed his lips over Binney's hair. "You're cute. Do you feel a bit like a kangaroo wearing that pouch?"

She laughed, rubbing her cheek against the flannel of his shirt. "At the store I said wet wipes were the best invention known to parents everywhere. Today it's a toss-up between them and this front pack. I gave Rex a bath this morning in his new tub. I wish you could have seen him kick and coo. He loved it."

He stopped and pressed his forehead to hers. "Binney, you shouldn't get so attached to him. Before I fell asleep something hit me that none of us brought up. Someplace, Rex has a real dad. After those DNA tests today we need to track down his aunt and wring more information out of her."

"She swore you were his father, Rio. Since it's obvious the midwife thought so, too, the only other person who'd really know is…dead. I know you're sure in your mind, but I can't imagine two women would cook up a scheme to…to do what? Later show up and scam money out of you? Are you secretly rich?"

"Lord, no. Do I need an appointment for the DNA test? I definitely want it done today if possible." Rio held back again at the bathroom door. Binney had yet to cover his cervical collar in plastic wrap.

She did that efficiently even with the baby kicking his feet and moving his arms. "No appointment needed as far as I know. After breakfast we'll go to the drop-in lab near the hospital. I was thinking, too, after I went to bed—" she passed him his shaver, but met his eyes in the mirror "—while we're in town I think we should visit the family clinic next door and have Rex checked by a pediatrician. I combed through the notes left by his aunt. Lindsey's midwife pronounced him in good condition. That's no more a bona fide exam than her note of birth is truly legal. I'll pay for it, Rio," she rushed to say.

"How would that look? I'll pay. Now let me get cleaned up so we can eat."

"Okay. You seem testy today. Be extra careful getting in and out of the shower," she said and ran her hands down his chest after she tucked the ends of the plastic wrap under the fat neck collar.

"I'm not testy at you." He looped his arms around her and the baby. Pulling her close, he brushed yet another a kiss across her bangs. "None of this mess is your fault," he said through a big sigh. "I am doing better, but stick close outside. I'll holler if I need you. After those exercises you did with my hand yesterday, it feels more limber. But my grip's still not a hundred percent."

She couldn't resist rubbing his prickly whiskers. "Your full strength will come back. Keep working that hand with the squeezy ball Dr. Darnell gave you."

As she always did, Binney left the door ajar and paced outside. This time she hummed to Rex, trying not to place too much importance on the couple of casual kisses Rio had delivered. One, after all, was to the top of her head. The other on her forehead—like an uncle with a favored niece. Not at all like a lover.

Soon, though, as happened with more regularity of late, her heart stumbled when Rio finally emerged scrubbed clean and shaven. No matter how many times she warned herself to view him as just as another patient, she too frequently experienced an unravelling of once tightly controlled emotions. Especially because he still needed her to button his shirts, and in doing it for him her fingers brushed his sculpted chest, sending her stuttering heart into overdrive.

From the smug gleam in his eyes, she knew he felt it, too.

Except for a couple of haphazard kisses, Rex's arrival had stalled the earlier ardor that had been developing between them. Binney feared she could be mostly to blame, because she wasn't able to believe Rio's denial. Rex seemed tangible proof that he'd tomcatted around. And it harkened back to the old days when every girl in their high school fawned over the McNabb twins, and they'd both cut a wide swath she knew for a fact. At least it'd been widely reported by those in the know.

AFTER BREAKFAST THEY went outside to Rio's pickup. From the passenger's seat, he phoned JJ. "We're leaving for the lab as soon as Binney installs the car seat in my truck. We left Tag in the house. I've no idea how long we'll be gone. Binney thinks we should have Rex checked by a doctor while we're in town."

"I feel for your predicament, Rio. Good luck with the test. Touch base when you get back."

"I will." Closing his cell phone, Rio dropped it on the console. He didn't need good luck for a test for which he already knew what the results would be.

He just needed results ASAP. And then he needed to get the baby to his rightful relatives.

"ISN'T THIS A glorious morning?" Binney asked a few minutes after they were under way. "I love how the first pop of sunlight filters through all the live oak trees around here and turns your private road into pure fantasyland."

"I'd like it better if I viewed the sun rising over the foothills while I'm out at dawn breaking a new horse."

"Rio, you can't think of climbing on a bucking horse for at least a year after Dr. Darnell releases you. Released won't mean your bones are as good as new. Not for a long time. Maybe I shouldn't be so blunt, but you hate the help you need now. Another accident akin to the last might leave you paralyzed."

"Dr. Layton was clear about that the first day he examined me. But JJ and I gentle our horses from the time they're foals by care in handling so they don't grow up to buck."

"Sorry, I just assumed…"

"It takes longer because a horse's inclination is to fight a bit and saddle. The most stubborn ones we take out into the pond where they can't buck when we're teaching them to bear our full weight. It's an old-time method true cowboys prefer."

"I like the sound of that practice. See, that's why you'll be a great dad. Kids do better with patience and understanding rather than criticism or punishment, too."

"I'm not going to be a dad, Binney. At least not anytime soon."

His flat denunciation ended their conversation.

On arriving at the lab some fifteen minutes later, Binney loaded Rex into the front pack again. Then she assisted Rio into the wheelchair she had muscled out of the pickup bed.

"I wish I could walk in on my own power."

"I know you do. I'm sorry the sidewalk is cobblestone."

Because she was familiar with the lab, they bypassed several steps and were soon ushered in to see a technician.

"That's quite a story," Sam Hartman, the lab technician, said, ending with a soft whistle. "Okay, so here's the deal. I'll swab the baby's saliva. But if you want the best, most accurate results, sir, I'll take a drop of your blood," he told Rio. "I recommend having a forensic DNA even though there are cheaper models. Forensic reports stand up in court."

"Court?" Frown lines gathered between Rio's eyebrows. "Do the best one, but I don't see why it'd come to that. Uh…how fast can I expect results?" he asked as Sam swabbed a spot with alcohol then pricked his finger.

"If we weren't backed up with police department work you'd have results in three to five days. Because Binney is a hospital employee I'll do my best to expedite this. However, be forewarned, it'll likely take seven to ten days."

Rio glanced at Binney. "That's better than my

ranch hand thought. He figured two weeks. As you might guess I'm anxious about the results."

"You said the aunt didn't give you much pertinent information on the baby's mother. Have you checked online to see if anyone posted her obit?" Sam asked, stripping off his gloves and donning a new pair before running a sterile cotton swab inside Rex's mouth.

The baby made a face, and Binney put him on her shoulder to rub his back. "I never thought about an obituary. We stopped here first, Sam, but next we're going over to the walk-in clinic to have the baby seen. His aunt didn't indicate whether he'd been checked at birth by a pediatrician. She came and left so fast I admit I never asked a lot of questions I should have."

Sam broke the swab off, corked the tube, labeled it, then rubber-banded it with Rio's small vial of blood. "If I were in your shoes I'd move heaven and earth to track the woman who left the baby. I think she could be charged with neglect for leaving him with a total stranger. I mean, you two have no idea, for instance, if he's had the hepatitis shot they give at birth now."

"I trust his birth date is correct, so he won't start routine shots for another month." Binney sounded confident as she tucked Rex back into his pack and secured him with the Velcro straps.

"Hep is now given at birth and again at one month." Sam walked with them to the door and then touched Rio's shoulder. "I saw your rodeo accident on TV. Add this problem, you're having a helluva year, man."

Rio pursed his lips. "I've definitely had better."

Outside, Binney asked him how he was holding up after she bumped his wheelchair over the lip of the door as they left the lab. "I'd suggest you wait in the pickup while I go down to the clinic, except I have no authority to have Rex examined."

"And I do?"

"By virtue of your name at the bottom of the midwife's delivery note, I think so. I brought it." She patted her pocket.

"Even if it's total bullshit?" He huffed out a breath. "I know you've no more hand in this mess than me, so let's just go get him examined, okay?"

"Rex isn't to blame for any of this, either. Quit looking at him as if he's poison."

"I'm not. He's a cute tyke. But he's not my son," Rio said for the umpteenth time.

Following that exchange they covered the distance to the clinic in total silence. A sign on the door read Mother and Infant Care Clinic. Binney struggled to open the door and back in with Rio's wheelchair. This time she jarred him twice.

"I wish we'd brought my crutches. I hate people thinking I'm a complete invalid."

And once inside, Rio turned out to be the only male in the waiting room. His condition earned sympathetic glances from other moms and staff, which he seemed to abhor.

In as much as it was a clinic for low-income families and those without insurance, it took a longer-than-normal consultation with several clerical staff to register Rex. Even as quietly as Binney tried to speak after explaining her role in being the one to fill out the paperwork, clerical questions caused many in the room to eye them with interest.

"I'm glad to be away from prying eyes," Rio muttered once they were shown into a room, and the nurse who'd undressed, weighed and measured Rex left them alone.

"I know you hate all of this," Binney said. "This won't be the last time you have to tell the story even if the DNA comes back in your favor."

"What do you mean, if? When it shows I'm not related, I'm done. Like it or not the next step will be to contact county social services. Are you prepared for that?"

Binney glanced away. "You've no idea the grilling we'll both be subjected to from their social workers." She would have fleshed that out further, but a doctor swept into the room, cutting off their private conversation.

"I'm Dr. Bernard." She nodded to each of them. "You two and this little guy have quite a tall tale, according to our intake staff," she murmured. Warming her stethoscope on her lab coat, she set it on Rex's chest. He kicked and waved his arms throughout his examination.

"I understand you're a registered nurse," Dr. Bernard said, casting an eye toward Binney after she sat down at a desk computer, where she struck a series of keys.

"I'm currently doing private duty nursing for Mr. McNabb. Anytime I'm between field jobs I schedule shifts with City Hospital. Mostly in ER."

The doctor studied Rio a moment, but her scrutiny again shifted to Binney. "How much longer will your current position last?"

Her heart dived. "I don't know for sure. Maybe a couple of weeks." She slanted her gaze toward Rio.

"I hope to lose the clavicle brace at my next doctor's visit," he provided. "That only leaves wearing the collar part-time for a once-cracked vertebrae that my orthopedic doc said is knitting. My broken left hand is weak, 'cause they just removed the cast. But I have a therapy ball that should help."

Binney quickly added for him, "He'll be able to get around his house once he has strength enough in that wrist to fully operate his crutches." She smiled at him and slipped her hand between Rio's neck collar and shoulder, pressing lightly. "I'll be at the ranch until his orthopedic doctor releases him," she said to the pediatrician.

"I was just wondering who'll handle the baby's care when you're gone. Also, who will bring him in for his immunizations?" As she talked, the doctor got up again and examined Rex's eyes, ears, throat, fingers and toes. Then she went back to the computer and typed some more.

"Someone will," Binney said with all the assurance of a person who knew when actually she didn't.

"Just write down the date you want him brought in again."

The doctor nodded. "For all it sounds like he's been through, he's a fine boy. The formula you listed provides essential vitamins. Add rice cereal at six weeks. Routine shots begin at two months. I think we'll skip a hepatitis shot today since we don't know if he had the first in the series. They're recommended at birth and four weeks, but can be started later. Pick up a copy of my report at the desk and schedule his next visit. It's easy to cancel if things change." The last statement she made directly to Rio. Then she hit Send on the computer, closed out the screen and walked to the door. "I hope whatever happens, he ends up in a loving home."

Binney's lips trembled as she restored Rex's clothes. She avoided Rio until she lifted the baby to strap him in her front pack and their eyes collided. It surprised her to note Rio's gray eyes were cloudy as if sad, and his mouth appeared pinched with concern. "What's wrong?" she asked, crossing to him.

"Just because he's not my son doesn't mean I want him tossed into a stream of unwanted kids." He scraped his right hand through his hair, leaving it standing on end. "We need to track down his aunt. She's the only one with answers."

"We don't have her name. Maybe she's a Cooper, but who knows. I know she abdicated all responsibility. Frankly, I don't understand how locating his aunt tells us anything more than what she already said to me."

"We'd better go," Rio said unhappily. "They probably need this room."

They left and Binney swung past the window bearing a sign that read Check Out Here. Since it was essentially a free clinic, there still seemed to be a suggested amount for a visit along with a recommended payment on a sliding scale for those who could afford something. She swiped her credit card and typed in the full amount.

"Thank you." The clerk smiled and tore off a receipt she gave Binney. "Here's the baby's report. Dr. Bernard wants to see him when he's two months old." The woman scrolled to her calendar and offered two possible dates.

Binney pocketed the receipt, passed Rio the report and blindly chose the first date knowing it was unlikely she'd be the one coming back.

"Why did you pay the bill?" Rio grumbled as they headed out.

"It didn't amount to a tenth of what you laid out on his supplies." Wedging open the outer door she somehow managed to get the wheelchair, herself and the baby out without assistance even though she banged her elbow hard enough on the door frame that for a moment it went numb.

At Rio's pickup she boosted him into the front passenger seat then buckled Rex into his car seat directly behind Rio. She rushed to the rear of the pickup and nearly fell over backward trying to lift the heavy wheelchair up and over the tailgate.

A Good Samaritan exiting an insurance office detoured to help.

"Thank you." She set blocks under the wheels so the chair wouldn't slide, and offered a head-bob again when the stranger closed the gate and shook it to make sure it was shut tight.

"I saw you put your husband and baby in the truck. Little lady, you need to install a lift or you'll end up needing one of these yourself."

His perfunctory smile blunted the warm rush of pleasure Binney felt hearing Rio termed her spouse and Rex her child. "Uh, his injury is only temporary," she stammered, thanking the man yet again before fumbling pickup keys out of her pocket.

He tipped his cowboy hat, walked away, and she dropped her keys twice on the way to climb in the driver's door.

"Who's the dude who stopped to yak? I hope he's somebody important enough to leave me with a crying baby I can't turn around to check on?" Rio was plainly miffed.

"Only a nice man who took pity on me. He helped me with your wheelchair. Sorry, I didn't hear Rex." She twisted over the console and gave the baby a pacifier she'd bought the previous night with all the other baby items. "He's due for a bottle, but I'm sure you're hungry, too. It won't take that long to get back to the Lonesome Road." She started the pickup and jockeyed out of the parking space.

"That woman who dropped him off has made us

snipe at each other, Binney. I hate it. We got along great before," Rio declared.

"If we credit her with recognizing that she couldn't raise her sister's baby, Rio, it might be easier. I don't see any reason for us to have cross words over this. Should I have thrown him and the tote bags of stuff back at her?"

"Of course not." Reaching across the console, he traced Binney's arm with fingertips of his once-bad hand. "You've assumed the lion's share of my care and his. I'll pay you extra."

"That's not necessary. Dogs, cats and kids are all factored into the price you're already paying me." Her eyes leaked tears. She didn't want extra money. She wanted Rio to accept Rex. And if she was honest, her.

"Well, when we set the contract it was just me and Tag."

"I know, but you forked out a lot at the store. And you're going to be slow assuming ranch duties for quite a while after you no longer need me."

"That reminds me. JJ said we have a buyer coming today for a colt and filly. Half of our mares are due to foal any day. If I get in shape to help train them, sales will be better than we've ever seen. It's what I've dreamed of since I bought the ranch."

"The doctor said you've done fantastic for the scope of your injuries. I realize it's hard not to get impatient, but keep following your doctor's orders. Don't overdo."

"It is hard when I watch you put together a crib,

that swing thing, a car seat, and you're forced to lift my wheelchair. Darnell said I'd have to wear this stupid neck collar for a year if I return to light work around the ranch. He and Layton said I shouldn't think of ever competing in a rodeo again. Not even on the working cowboy's circuit, which I'd hoped to do."

"So what? Is competing and winning so important?"

Rio screwed up his face. "Watching you work while I'm sidelined isn't manly."

Amid a full-throated laugh she couldn't contain, Binney braked in a cloud of dust in front of the house. "Rio, I promise if you only stand by a corral, anyone looking at you will call you manly." She hopped out, took down the wheelchair and hustled everyone into the house, where they were greeted effusively by Tag. It pleased her all the same when she caught Rio smiling for the first time that day.

She started to help him to his bed, but he stayed her with a hand.

"I want a TENS session to hopefully hurry the healing process on my neck. Then if you'll hand me my laptop, I'm going to take Sam Hartman's suggestion and hunt for Lindsey Cooper's obituary."

"Okay. I'll feed Rex and then decide what to fix for our lunch."

Not long after they'd both settled silently in opposite chairs, Rio called to Binney. "Success! I found it. The obit. Come read it with me."

She set aside Rex's empty bottle and tucked him

into his bouncy swing. She started its music box and stepped over Tag to go sit on the arm of Rio's rocker. "It's not very helpful," she said, squinting at the screen. "We already knew her name, age and that she has an unnamed older sister. Clever how whoever provided this information really didn't give particulars. It doesn't even say she died from complications of childbirth, or say where she worked."

"Yeah." Rio pinched his lower lip. "Also there's an unnamed parent, their dad, who apparently lives in an Alzheimer facility in Arkansas. With no city listed. Not that he could be of any assistance if he has dementia. Look, there is a photo of her…Lindsey." He scrolled to a black-and-white headshot. "Too grainy to be of any use." Rio started to hit delete.

"Wait. Print it," Binney urged. "It's clear enough to see she has long dark hair and is pretty."

"She's a liar," Rio declared emphatically.

Binney traced a finger along Rio's rock-hard jaw. "One day it may be Rex's only connection to his birth mother. Something like that would have meant the world to me," she said, gazing over at the baby with shimmering eyes.

Relaxing his shoulders, Rio pressed her palm against his cheek. "I remember one of my mom's favorite sayings—the Lord works in mysterious ways. Maybe that daft woman brought Rex here so you would be his spirit guide through the system."

"His what?" Binney sat near enough to inhale the scent of Rio's aftershave, and it rattled her. She removed her hand and scrubbed away tears.

"A friend, a Native American bronc rider, claimed his grandfather sent him a spirit guide to watch over him on the rodeo circuit. I guess I'm mixing religious beliefs. Spirit guide, guardian angel or whatever we want to call it, you're the one with experience to take care of Rex, and you've gone through losing your parents at his age. I figure no matter what happens you can maybe stay in touch and help him understand."

"I rather like the idea of being Rex's spirit guide. Most likely it's you, though. I keep pointing out, you're the one Lindsey apparently named as his father. Send that article to print and I'll clip it to the copy of his birth record. If it comes to tracing his roots further, every snippet of information will help." Suddenly an emotional mess, she leaned down and kissed Rio. She aimed for his cheek, but being tippy on the chair arm, hit his lips, which made her hot and tingly all over.

He tried to deepen the kiss, but Binney slid off the arm of the chair. "Uh, sorry. I wasn't making a move on you, Rio. It's all the comparisons between how Rex and I were both abandoned. I just want you to want him." She quickly changed the subject. "Do you see how Rex is loving his swing? I…uh…will run in and fix us some lunch."

Rio attempted to maintain a hold on her arm, but she disengaged easily from his still-weak left hand.

THROUGHOUT THE NEXT few days Binney took real heart in Rio's sprouting interest in Rex. Where in the beginning he'd acted gruff, now she often caught him talking to the baby as if he were explaining things to Tag. He took turns feeding Rex without complaint and grinned watching him kick his legs and gurgle in the swing. Rio also seemed to love how Rex intently stared at Contessa, the pregnant mare, when the three of them took daily walks out to the corral.

Binney couldn't help it, her feelings for Rio expanded, too. To the extent that one afternoon she blurted without thinking, "In high school most of my girlish daydreams centered on Ryder before he dumped me. Before that he stood out larger than life. But you're a good man, Rio McNabb."

Rio started to speak, but Rex cried his *I-need-changing* cry, and she hurried off with a dry diaper, neglecting to confess that it was hard to understand now, how back then Rio flew under her radar. Thinking back, Ryder had always had smug arrogance she'd misconstrued as charm.

RIO SAT IN his recliner with the electronic unit intended to heal his vertebrae. Since he had the use of both hands to type now, he worked on ranch records. His fingers stilled and he thought about telling Binney why he and his brother weren't speaking. But his folks thought he should forgive and forget the incident even though they, too, placed more blame on his twin. But did he really want her to feel sorry for him, or take his side against his twin?

No, that wasn't his way even if he was on the verge of falling in love with his private duty nurse.

What he really wanted was for Binney to see him as a whole man. Not as an invalid who needed her nursing care.

Starting that moment, Rio redoubled his efforts to do more to help himself. He spent extra time getting around using only his crutches. Whether he wanted to or not, he needed to prepare for the day Binney would leave the ranch. But he honestly didn't know if he wanted it to be sooner rather than later. And if she left before he turned Rex over to someone else, he couldn't care for a baby alone. But as it stood, no way could he share his deepest feelings for her until he was able to offer himself on equal ground.

Anytime Binney left the house to go after the mail, Rio phoned Las Vegas casinos personnel offices, asking if they'd employed Lindsey Cooper. With so many casinos and so little time, he hadn't so far made any inroads at all.

ON FRIDAY, REX was napping and Rio and Binney were in the middle of exercising his left hand when a call from the lab popped up on Rio's cell phone. They both tensed while he answered.

"Yes, this is Rio McNabb. Oh, hi, Sam. You have my test results already? Fantastic, give me the good news." Rio flashed Binney a grin.

As quickly, he frowned. "You can't give me the results over the phone? Ah… I don't see any reason why we can't come to the lab now." He waited for Binney's nod. "We'll head out ASAP and be there in half an hour or so."

"It's odd he couldn't provide you a simple yes or no." She capped the cream she'd been rubbing into Rio's wrist and hand.

"I agree. But he said they have to show me the graphs. I trust they have good reason."

Tag wasn't happy to be left behind, but Rex didn't appear to mind being awakened and hauled out to the pickup. He loved slapping the string of rattles attached to his car seat.

In spite of the baby's happy gurgles, tension arced between Binney and Rio.

"It's almost over, Rio," she said haltingly, her hands flexing around the steering wheel. "If you'd like after we finish at the lab we can stop and see if Dr. Darnell thinks you're able to shed the clavicle brace, providing you continue to use the neck collar for limited tasks around the ranch. That way I can leave and you'll be free again."

"How do you figure?"

"Well, you expect the tests to absolve you of fatherhood. You'll call social services, and once you no longer need anything except the neck collar, you won't need me underfoot."

A coldness gripped Rio. Binney had taken hold of his heart, and so had the cute baby with the chubby cheeks and sparkling dark eyes. That came as a shock to him.

"I know Rex and I won't share DNA," he finally said, not venturing that until Binney motored up to the lab and found a parking spot. "It'll still take time to work out handing him over to social services. I'll still need your help with him. So you won't be leaving right away, Binney."

Even as they left the vehicle and he was able to walk into the lab using his crutches, he was seized by a moment of panic where he wanted to grab Binney and Rex and go home. His steps slowed markedly. He stopped altogether when he heard Binney give his name to a receptionist.

She glanced around, her arms steadying the baby in the front pack. "Rio, are you okay? They said Sam's expecting you, so we can go straight on back." She returned to where he sagged on his crutches.

He stroked the pudgy hand of the happily kicking boy. "Suddenly I'm not sure I'm ready to hear that some unknown man is Rex's father."

Binney rose on tiptoe and brushed a kiss across Rio's trembling lips. "More than all the other times you've denied the possibility, your sadness now convinces me you've told the truth about not knowing Lindsey Cooper. If that's any consolation, I guess it comes too late since Sam's waiting for us at the door."

Hauling in a deep breath, Rio hobbled past her.

Inside the lab workroom, Sam directed them past a couple of other technicians to a waist-high table, where he spread out a set of papers. "Examine these four lines closely, Rio. Placed side by side they show that you and Rex share several specific genetic markers."

"Impossible." Rio huffed out a massive breath. At the same time his body bucked and he dropped one of his crutches.

Binney moved quickly to his side. She circled his waist with one arm, murmuring, "Rio, your heart is galloping and I can feel your legs shaking. Sam, he needs to sit down." Looking around, she pulled over a stool.

"Good. You sit, Rio. I'm not finished," Sam said, drawing their attention to two new papers he laid on the table.

Binney guided Rio to be seated as Sam continued pointing at lines. "These graphs show variants." His finger tracked four lines that didn't intersect with matching segments marked with Rio's name.

"You're saying those aren't differences due to his mother?" Binney asked.

"These outliers are female chromosomes belonging to his mother." The technician traced green lines that did align with those of the baby.

An older man with graying hair and glasses came from across the room to their table. "I've been doing this work for thirty years, Mr. McNabb. And I'm the second geneticist Sam had go over these results. Have you had cancer?" he inquired abruptly of Rio.

"Never."

"He's recently been in the hospital after a bad accident he sustained at a rodeo," Binney supplied. "With as many MRIs, blood work and X-rays as he's undergone, his doctors would have spotted cancer. Is there another lab, say in a bigger city, where Rio can be retested?" she asked.

Sam pinched his lower lip as he eyed Binney. "Any forensic technique has limitations. Of course you're free to go to San Antonio or Dallas. But we had three experts study these tests. All were puzzled by the anomalies. One of our geneticists said it might be a result of their age difference or other family discrepancies."

"Ryder," Rio said, reaching out to grip Binney's arm.

The older technician had walked away, but turned back when Binney said excitedly, "You may be onto something, Rio. Now I remember. In my last year of nursing school I had a lab class where the instructor showed us slides on cutting-edge blood studies being done on identical twins. That was a few years ago, but I'm sure he showed samples of variations they'd found when it had been commonly thought identical twins' blood bore exactly the same properties." Binney threw up her hands. "Is it likely? Why wouldn't the mother have had Ryder's name?"

"This screwup is damned sure something my brother would do."

Sam Hartman broke in. "If you'd told me you have an identical twin we would have had a probable explanation for the marker variations. You need to contact him and ask him to be tested. Or, if he's the little guy's biological dad, maybe he'll just tell you."

Rio gritted his teeth. "I don't have his phone number. I'm sure my mom does. I think she and Dad are due back from their trip this week. I have no idea how to begin trying to explain this to her. Maybe I can just ask for Ryder's number. Let's go,

Binney." He struggled to stand. "I could wring Ryder's neck."

Although she appeared a bit dazed, she assisted him.

"Will you get back to me if you learn anything from your brother that explains the marker differences? Or someone could send us a sample of his blood to test and compare." Sam pressed Rio. "I can tell Binney's still puzzled. However, if true it'd help us to ask more questions on our future DNA application forms."

"I'll call you. It's definitely possible," Rio said testily.

Chapter Ten

Binney hurriedly thanked Sam for the speedy way they'd returned the tests before she dashed after Rio, who made a beeline out of the lab.

She caught up to him and begged him to slow down before he tripped and fell. "I am as confused as ever. Why would Lindsey not have given her sister and the midwife Ryder's name?"

"I know you used to think he walked on water. You'd believe this if you knew why he and I haven't spoken for almost four years in spite of my parents doing their best to smooth things over."

He pulled away from Binney on the way to the parking lot. Propelling himself ahead of her, he threw his crutches into the back of the pickup, and swore when he couldn't climb into the passenger seat without her assistance.

"Rio, stop it. Please. You're going to hurt yourself again." She tried unsuccessfully to calm him and ended up boosting him up into the passenger seat in an ungainly fashion. Then when he stubbornly said nothing, she quietly buckled Rex in his car seat and made sure he had his pacifier. It didn't take a genius to read Rio's stormy countenance as she backed out and began the drive to the ranch. What did it all mean for Rex? It hurt to think of the possibilities.

"Listen, Rio, I'm sorry I mentioned you and Ryder being identical twins. I lampooned both of you in front of Sam and the other techs. You traded identities as kids to prank the teachers. You're both grown up now."

"One of us is," Rio countered. "Let me tell you about our last dispute." His lips turned down as he rubbed his chin. "We were both at a PRCA rodeo in Denver. Ryder and some buddies shared a ritzy hotel suite. Someone in the group had won high points and big money bull riding. They threw a party and trashed the room. I'd gone on to Wyoming when I got served a summons for a court date in Colorado. It turned out my dear brother used my name on the hotel registration form. I denied being there, but the manager picked me out of a photo lineup. I was forced to pay damages and a fine in order to have my case acquitted. My folks contacted him, and Ryder paid me back, but he thought it was funny. He said he did it because he was afraid the party would get rowdy and he didn't want to reflect badly on bull riders and the PRC. So…do I put it past him to lie to a woman about his name? Hell, no!"

Binney digested his story bit by bit, but she didn't know what to say, because it sounded so terrible.

Rio slumped in his seat. "My brother has always been brash and arrogant, and more so once he started getting a big name in the PBR. He's a hard-charging partier and a womanizer. He'll never change."

Letting the reverberation of his words fade, Binney probed gently, "Rio, you admit you haven't seen each other in almost four years. Maybe he was egged on by his friends to pull that stunt at the hotel. You've matured. Until you talk to him you can't be positive he's involved in this. Remember the older geneticist said health reasons could cause DNA anomalies."

"Why are you standing up for Ryder?" Rio growled. "I tell you there is no other explanation. In fact, I should have thought of him myself."

Binney opened her mouth to refute that her hope about the truth had anything to do with Ryder. Really she didn't want sweet baby Rex to land in the center of a family squabble. And she didn't want Ryder to be Rex's biological father, because everything Rio said about his twin being arrogant and brash was true.

But before she could tell Rio, she pulled into the ranch and noted a strange vehicle, a dusty green SUV sitting where she usually parked. "Hey, maybe Rex's aunt had second thoughts and had someone bring her back here."

Straightening, Rio followed her finger. "That's my dad's Range Rover. I wonder what they're doing here." He flung open his door before Binney had shut off the engine.

A pretty, vibrant woman Binney recalled having seen at the twins' high school sports events rushed out of the house and down the steps followed by a tall man only slightly gray at the temples. *Rio's dad.*

A suddenly shy observer, Binney spared a moment to appreciate how much Rio resembled his father. She cataloged how handsome Rio would still be in his retirement years.

"Mom," Rio shouted. "When did you get back from Australia? And why are you here?" He slid out of the cab and teetered. It forced him to hang on to the door so he didn't fall.

Linda McNabb rushed to steady her son. "We got home and our neighbor gave us several news articles about your terrible accident. I was so worried we came to see how badly you'd fared. We've only been here a short while. Your dad was just going out to the barns to see if that's where you and JJ were."

"Hand me my crutches and I'll explain a few things. I'm really glad you're here."

His mother took the crutches her husband had lifted out of the pickup bed. "We've been inside." She passed the crutches to Rio. "What else has happened while we were gone? Care to fill us in on all of the baby stuff strewn around the living room?"

Rio stopped at the front fender. "Uh, will you get the baby from his car seat? It's behind where I sat. We'll go inside and talk about a bunch of stuff." He still felt rocked by the news from the test, and let down by Binney's willingness to abet Ryder.

His mother turned and opened the back door. Plainly shocked, she nevertheless leaned in and unbuckled the baby. In doing so her curious gaze strayed to where Binney remained unmoving in the driver's seat.

"Ah, hello." Grabbing Rex, his mom whispered a tad too loudly, "Rio, is she the baby's mother? It appears you have a whole lot of explaining to do."

"What? No, that's Binney Taylor, my home care nurse. She's been taking care of the baby, too. Now, though, if you and Dad can stay on a couple of weeks until I get cleared by the orthopedic doctor, Binney can leave ASAP. I know that's her wish, because she mentioned it."

"Sure, honey." Still wearing a confused expression, his mother shut the back door of the king cab. She cradled the baby and stepped around Tag, who'd bounded out of the house with them. "If you need us, Rio, of course we'll stay awhile. Right?" She deferred to her husband, who shrugged and nodded.

Binney emerged around the hood only to have Rio say, "Hear that? Earlier you sounded more than ready to be on your way. Now you can go. I'll cut your check while you pack."

Shock over the rapidity of how everything was ending stole Binney's breath. She slowly trailed Rio and his family to the house feeling worse than a fifth wheel as she heard him pouring out the story of how he came to have Rex.

Once inside, Rio's mute father stood behind the chairs where his wife and son sat. Linda in a recliner still holding the baby, Rio at the desk, where he took out the ranch checkbook.

Binney circumvented the group and went straight to her bedroom. It was with a leaden heart that she began folding clothes into her saddlebags. As yet she hadn't heard Rio mention Ryder.

Tag loped into her room, rubbed against her and whined.

She hugged him before she hefted her things, went out and snatched the check Rio waved at her. "Dad's going to call Ryder and put him on speaker phone, but you don't have to stay. No matter what he says you'd take his side." Impatiently, Rio waved her away.

"I didn't, I wouldn't…" She tried to deny that by suggesting he give his twin a chance to answer questions meant she was favoring Ryder. "Okay, think what you will. For Rex's sake I hope Ryder has changed," she said, eyes passing over Rio and his silent folks. "In the time I've cared for you and the baby, believe me, I've completely shed any rose-colored glasses when it comes to your brother."

Tightening his lips, Rio muttered, "Not fifteen minutes ago you tried counseling me that he's matured. You know what, I'd rather not discuss Ryder with you anymore. Goodbye, Binney. Uh, thanks for all of your help. If you need references I'll provide them, of course."

She hadn't reached the outer door when Ryder's voice boomed into the room. She badly wanted to stay and hear what he had to say for himself. However, staying would only make Rio more certain she still had some lingering interest in his twin.

She'd cried while packing, but now her tears ran unchecked. At the door she had to shove Tag back with a quick scratch to his chest so he couldn't follow her out. Wiping at her eyes, she stumbled to the barn to get the Harley that she hadn't ridden in the five weeks she'd been at the ranch.

She heard JJ out back working with the horses, and was thankful he didn't emerge to chat. Blotting her eyes, she secured her saddlebags, picked up her helmet and wheeled her bike out to the lane. Once there, she gazed again at the ranch she'd come to love. Before she became overwhelmed with sorrow and regret, she donned her helmet, slung a leg over the Harley and stomped down on the kick-starter. She was very thankful her bike roared to life and ran smoothly without choking. She wasted no time in peeling away.

Twice before she reached the main highway she had to stop and soak in the scenery. The second time she remembered she hadn't kissed the baby goodbye. And Rio—darn it all, he filled her hurting heart. True he had blustered and had ordered her to leave, but she would bet all she had in the world it was because he was hurting, too. Probably there was nothing to be done about that. At least not now. Maybe never.

INSIDE THE RANCH house Rio's dad spoke to his other son, letting him know they'd returned from Australia and were currently at the Lonesome Road.

Moving closer to Rio, his mother touched his arm. "Did you notice your nurse's red, puffy eyes? I think your sending her away so abruptly made her cry.

Now you don't look so good, either. What, besides thinking Ryder falsely used your name and got some woman pregnant, is going on?"

"Nothing! Dad, ask Ryder about Lindsey Cooper. That's the name of the baby's mother. Her sister told Binney something went wrong in her home birth and Lindsey died on the way to the hospital. See if Ryder knows that."

Rex started to fuss. Rio's mother swayed with him, but he only sobbed louder.

"There are diapers in one of those bags. And he may be hungry, Mom, although I've never heard him fuss so much." Rio cupped a hand around the baby's head and it did lessen his sobs.

Tag ran over, set his chin on Rio's knee and whimpered. Then he ran back and forth to the door as if wanting someone to bring Binney back.

"Stop it, Tag. Uh, maybe I was too hasty in sending Binney away," Rio stammered. "Mom, can you take Tag and Rex into the kitchen? There's premixed formula in the cupboard. And kibble for Tagalong. I need to hear what Ryder tells Dad."

She obliged, although it was plain she wanted to stay and listen. She herded the lop-eared dog into the kitchen.

Rio heard his father ask if Ryder knew a woman in Las Vegas named Lindsey Cooper.

Rio fidgeted through his brother's lengthy pause. So long he wondered if his twin had hung up.

Finally the man on the other end of the call responded. "Why? Geez, has she turned up at the ranch? Tell Rio she's a leech. I never thought she'd go so far as to hunt him down. I swear it."

"Rio had a horse buck over on him. Did you know that? And what about this Cooper woman? What's the story, Ryder?"

"I only recently heard about his accident when I was in Florida. I'm in Kansas City now. My next event is in Corpus Christi. I planned to swing by the ranch to see how he's doing. We're in the final phase leading up to the world championships, you know." He coughed. "Obviously Lindsey tracked Rio down. Warn him to not get mixed up with her. She's trouble with a capital *T*."

"How so?" asked the elder McNabb.

"Well, it's kind of convoluted. The best friend of a fellow bull rider dated her. He had filed for divorce from his wife, but they decided to get back together. Lindsey kept bugging him, threatening to call his wife to insist he really loved her. Our mutual friend Troy Pritchard wanted to help. Both guys insisted Lindsey was only in love with the idea of being attached to a rodeo cowboy. Troy asked if I'd invite her out and bust up her fixation on his pal. She was pretty, so I flirted some and then asked her out."

"And you used your brother's name?" his dad charged.

"No. I didn't claim to be Rio. As it turned out he'd just ridden in Vegas the previous week. Lindsey had watched his event and his win. Her casino and others, plus my hotel still had flyers all over with Rio's picture. She immediately thought I was him. I didn't tell her any different. We went out a few nights. The last evening we had dinner and drinks in my room. By then it was plain she was hell-bent on marrying a cowboy. Any cowboy. You all know I'm not the marrying kind. She did her best to wrangle my phone number, but I never gave it to her. If she's found Rio, I didn't help her."

Rob McNabb's voice hardened. "So, you did pretend to be him, though."

"Ah…yeah, in a way I did, because I never corrected her error." He laughed. "Rio was long gone to another event. I was blowing Las Vegas, too, so I figured what the hell!"

"The hell is, Ryder, you got Ms. Cooper pregnant. She had the baby and her sister and the midwife assumed he was the baby's dad. I hate to be the one to break the worst news. Lindsey died from complications and her sister dumped the baby in Rio's lap."

For several moments there was nothing but crackling on the speaker phone.

"She's dead? That's awful. I'd never wish that on her or anyone. Geez, you guys, it's not my kid. I don't like talking to my parents about my sex life, but the one night we did it, I used condoms. I always use protection."

His fury building, Rio shouted, "You dumb ass, your so-called protection failed. I had DNA testing. I knew I'd never met the woman. There were aberrations in the results, because while we share a lot, we don't have identical DNA."

"God, Rio, I had no idea. I'm sorry," Ryder said

in a raspy voice. "Listen, I was going to leave here in the morning. I'll take off now. I can be at the ranch by daylight. We have to talk. This can't happen. For the first time ever I'm high enough in the point standings that I'm within striking distance of being the next world bull-riding champion. Tell Mom I'll be there for breakfast."

The elder McNabb frowned at his phone. "Ryder. Ryder?" Looking up, he shook his head. "He hung up. No use calling him back, he won't pick up. It's good he's coming. But this is your ranch now, Rio. Are you okay with seeing him?"

"I don't know. I'm mad as hell, but I have the baby. The midwife wrote my name on her record. So, let him come. We have to get this resolved, Dad."

Linda McNabb entered the room having finally calmed the baby. "I heard some of that. Ryder needs to step up and take responsibility."

"Has he ever?" Rio asked bitterly, struggling to get out of the chair.

His dad pocketed his phone. "Linda, how did he turn out so damned self-centered? When the boys were teens, did we help Ryder out of one too many scrapes of his own making?"

"We did what we thought was right, Rob. This is especially egregious, but I can't not love him. He sounded shaken. Maybe this will teach him a lesson."

"I hope so. There's a baby who didn't ask for any of this. I still carry photos of you boys from about this baby's age, Rio." Rob got out his billfold and peeled out a folder of photographs. "Everyone thought you were cute as could be when you started mutton busting at the Abilene rodeo." He unfurled the packet under Rio's nose.

"Dad, don't. Ryder and I have been growing apart since…I don't really know when. I think that issue at the Denver hotel was the end for me." He sat in the rocker and reached out to take the baby. "This little guy deserves stability," he murmured, borrowing from what Binney said repeatedly. "Ryder didn't sound as if he'd be willing to raise this poor little bugger."

His mother set the now sleeping child in his arms. "You give all appearances of becoming attached, though."

"I guess so. Binney handled the lion's share caring for him, but I've helped." He gazed down on Rex and smiled when the baby cooed. "He's such a happy little guy."

His mom sat on the arm of his chair. "Honey, running a ranch is difficult in itself. You're battling injuries. Frankly I can't fathom what it'd be like to be a single dad on top of that."

"It's true, son. You can barely get around," Mr. McNabb said. "Maybe the nurse you had helping knows of a reputable adoption agency in town. It's not my druthers, but we need to look at what'd be best for the boy."

Rio shifted. His shoulders sagged. "I see you don't remember that Binney attended school with Ryder and me. She was abandoned as a baby and was never adopted. Agencies don't always find families, Dad.

And fostering didn't sound ideal in all cases, either. She doesn't like to talk about it, but I know Binney had a hard life. I want better for Rex."

"And so do we," Rob said, walking over to put his arm around his wife. "I say we set talk aside until Ryder gets here tomorrow. Linda, didn't you bring a cooler with some sandwiches?" He returned his wallet to his back pocket.

"I did. There wasn't much in the way of food in our condo after being gone a month. I hurriedly made and packed PB&J. You okay with that, Rio? I can put on a pot of coffee, too," his mother said.

"I can eat a sandwich. Although I'm not very hungry. Binney fixed bacon and waffles for breakfast. I ate a lot knowing we were going to get my lab results. That seems as if it happened ages ago," he said, gazing vacantly into space.

"Rob, if you put the baby in his swing and help Rio make his way into the kitchen, I'll go fix lunch." She hugged Rio and went toward the kitchen.

Rio's father bent down and scooped up the sleeping child. "Hey, tadpole, come to Grandpa."

Rio blinked. "It's true, Dad, you are Rex's real grandfather. Binney would've loved hearing you say that," Rio murmured as his father helped him out of the recliner. "She wanted him to belong someplace with a family who cared about him."

BINNEY RODE STRAIGHT into town from the ranch. She felt a need to shower away the sweat and dust from her ride. As a rule she would have stopped at the bank to deposit her earnings. Today angry stomach cramps brought on by being summarily dismissed left her too restless to even care about Rio's generous check. Had he paid her more because he felt guilty for the way he hustled her out? He ought to. She'd like to be a fly on the wall back at the ranch. She couldn't help but wonder how the conversation with Ryder McNabb had gone.

It wasn't her problem. It was time she marked the last weeks off as a bad experience.

As yet unable to face Mildred since her elderly friend was so perceptive, Binney got off her Harley a block from the apartment complex and pushed it to her assigned parking spot. Then she hiked up the back stairs, taking care to not jingle her keys lest Mildred hear.

She went straight to her bedroom, stripped off her clothes and stepped under a bracing warm spray. Once clean she wrapped in a big towel, fell back on her bed and stared at the ceiling. She was mad at herself for caring so much about Rio and the baby. For nearly her whole life all she'd wanted was to be a nurse. She was still that. Just because seeing Rio McNabb again had awakened old yearnings she'd had as a lonely teen, it really had no bearing on her future. The few hugs and kisses they'd shared meant nothing.

Sitting up, Binney unwound the towel. She hadn't believed Rio about not fathering Rex and she'd been wrong. She had tried to apologize, but he'd chosen not to listen. She needed to get over him, and fast.

Finally she donned clean clothes, but she chided herself for the way she'd all but fled Rio's ranch as if she was guilty of something. If his parents hadn't been there she would have argued and at least tried to make him understand that she could never back Ryder, not after the things he'd pulled on Rio. She was sorry to learn he was Rex's biological father. Did she wish he had grown up enough to man up? Yes, especially for Rex's sake. And for Rio's. They'd each stolen pieces of her heart.

But, damn it, Rio should have recognized where her concern and hope had sprung from. Falling for him had been a serious blunder.

Her heart ached as it hadn't ached in a very long time. She thought Rio had seen the real her and thought he liked her. Yet he couldn't kick her out of his life fast enough.

At least it didn't have anything to do with her nursing care. He'd offered her recommendations.

Knowing that didn't ease the pain in her heart.

But hadn't Lola Vickers cautioned her to not let herself get too attached to the people she did home health care for? Yet she'd done just that. Gotten attached to Rio and the baby. Even attached to his dog, for pity's sake. And the ranch. She loved the Lonesome Road.

This might be a wake-up call for her to quit home care and return to work in the hospital. The ER needed another full-time nurse. And with the variety of cases they dealt with, she shouldn't get bored.

Nor would she have any patient long enough to develop an attachment.

That's what she would do. And she wouldn't give herself any time to waffle. Scooping up her earnings and the key to her Harley, she left to deposit the check with Rio's name on it and go ask for her old nursing job back at the hospital. That should keep her busy enough to erase Rio McNabb from her mind and her heart.

Once she had secured another job, she'd go back and share the whole impossible-sounding story with Mildred.

Chapter Eleven

Later that afternoon, Rio and his folks took the baby and Tag on a journey out to see JJ and the horses. The outing didn't have the usual enjoyment for Rio. It wasn't Binney laughing and holding Rex up to see and pat Contessa.

He wasn't hungry for supper, because Binney didn't fix it and she wasn't around to play her guitar to help him and Rex relax and fall asleep that night.

In fact he barely slept at all.

His mom got up for Rex's 2:00 a.m. feeding. Tag padded over to his bed and whined, very likely because he couldn't find Binney. Damn, but Rio missed her and she hadn't even been gone a full day. He missed her smile. He missed her touch. He hadn't expected to feel so bereft.

EVERYONE ROSE EARLY the next morning, and Linda had pancakes and scrambled eggs ready when Ryder rolled up in his midnight blue Tesla. It was easy to see where he spent his winnings. Rio steeled himself for the visit.

His brother stalked into the house, removed his cowboy hat, looked around at his family and said, "I've thought about this horrific problem on the entire drive from KC. I hate that my protection failed and Lindsey had a baby. It's awful something happened and she died. But I've gotta be honest here. I've never wanted to be a husband or father. I don't have what it takes to settle down. You know that, Rio." His shifting gaze stopped on his twin.

Their father gestured toward the kitchen. "I suggest we discuss this over breakfast. Your mom has it ready. And Ryder, you shouldn't make a hard-and-fast decision before you've seen your son."

Ryder grimaced, tossed his hat on a chair and caused Tag to growl ominously. "Sorry," Ryder said. "I wanted to get that out from the get-go. Rio, you still don't look so good. You have to believe me when I say I didn't know about Lindsey being pregnant. I swear I didn't hear about your accident until I was at the rodeo in Kansas."

Linda McNabb collected the baby from his swing, put him in his infant seat and let her husband carry him to the kitchen table. He placed the seat where Ryder was forced to face the baby. His baby.

Rio, who'd thought all night about what he wanted to say to his wayward twin, held his tongue and brought up the rear. He waited until he'd had a bracing swig of coffee before he spoke. "I'm healing. Slower than I'd like. Frankly, I didn't expect to hear from you. Given our most recent history I'm surprised I didn't suspect you when the aunt showed up out of the blue and gave the baby to my home nurse, insisting he was mine."

His brother had the grace to look guilty. Only as their mother dished out food did Ryder take time to study the baby. "I probably should feel something for him, but I don't. It doesn't seem real. His mother was only a week's flirtation to me. Pop, can you and Mom adopt him or something? I'll send money toward his keep."

Linda passed her husband hot sauce for his eggs. "Ryder, we're retired. You know we live in a senior community. They don't allow children except for short visits. We're prepared to help out as grandparents, but eighteen years of parenting is your responsibility."

Ryder kept shaking his head and fiddling with his fork. "I can't."

"You jerk," Rio grated, slamming down the syrup pitcher. "I'll raise Rex providing you relinquish all rights. I want something airtight and legal. Oh, and a paragraph swearing you'll never impersonate me again."

"You mean that?" Ryder sounded too grateful, too quick. "I'll see a lawyer after breakfast. Maybe I don't have grounds to ask for anything, but can we keep this under wraps? The PBR doesn't like messy stuff dogging their riders. Rumor says you're leaving the PRCA for the RHAA. That means we'll never land in the same cities at the same time, bro."

"Don't bro me," Rio said through clenched teeth. "Your colossal nerve rubs me wrong. My injuries have very likely excluded me from all rodeo. I'm going to raise horses at the Lonesome Road. Get me custody papers. I'll claim Rex Quintin McNabb as my son, and you'll never be more than his uncle. Be real sure you can live with that."

"I can. I know he'll be better off with you, Rio. I promise I'll stay out of your life except for if we all end up at Mom and Dad's for holidays or something. Are you able to ride in a vehicle? If so, let's go see an attorney together. Not in Abilene, where we're known. We can go to Big Springs and have something drawn up. Dad can drive you home and I'll head on to Corpus Christi."

It was a quiet breakfast thereafter. Once Ryder phoned and booked an appointment with a lawyer for just prior to noon, Linda volunteered to stay behind with Rex and Tag.

Rob drove Rio in his pickup and Ryder led the way in his car. Rio spent most of the drive staring fixedly out the window.

It turned out after listening to the story and seeing the midwife's report, the lawyer had forms where all they had to do was fill in their names and affix signatures.

"Boys, it seems as if this covers everything pertinent," Rob said once they'd all read the document through. "Although, what about this line that says Ryder relinquishes forever all legal, moral and monetary obligations for Rex, who he admits he likely fathered. Shouldn't he have to pay support? This lets him totally off the hook."

"There's no likely about it. I have copies of the DNA tests. But, if I accept support won't that open the door for him to maybe one day change his mind and want paternity rights?" Rio asked.

"I swear I won't," Ryder said quietly. "I'm not currently and may never be father material. Even if I meet someone that I someday want to marry, I can't see it happening for years. Trust me, Rio." Ryder extended his hand.

Rio met his twin's eyes for several protracted moments before he accepted and clasped his hand. "My home care nurse knew us in high school. She went with me to get the DNA results. She said maybe you'd matured. I want to believe you have."

"This has had a sobering effect. You were never footloose like me. If I win this championship I want to travel and see the world." He fidgeted and finally asked, "Does this agreement mean you can't occasionally send Uncle Ryder photographs? Is it wrong for me to at least want to see he's doing okay?"

Rio glanced at the lawyer, who'd tipped back in his chair. The white-haired man pressed his fingers together. "Strictly speaking from my fifty years in family law, it's totally up to the guardian how much to share."

"I didn't think I'd be open to anything like that, but I am."

The elder McNabb smiled at his sons, and Ryder scribbled his name on the copies, followed by Rio, who did the same.

The three men exited the office carrying their respective folders. "Pop, will you keep this for me?" Ryder held out his folder. "I'd like it a lot if you all could come see me ride in the championships. Maybe that's too much to expect. It requires travel."

Rio leaned heavily on his crutches. "We'll see how I am in December. JJ and Rhonda are getting married then. If the wedding doesn't conflict with your event, maybe I can manage both. I do hope you win."

"Your mom and I will try to make it. Let us know the date." He and Rio watched Ryder climb in his Tesla and drive off before Rob helped Rio into the pickup.

"That was generous of you, son. I'm proud of you, but still disappointed in Ryder."

"You are? I think this time he'll try and make an effort to change some of his wild ways."

"If that wasn't all show for the lawyer."

"He's always wanted to be a superstar. Although that will make him more popular with rodeo groupies like Lindsey Cooper." Rio smoothed a hand over the hollows of his cheeks.

"It bothered me that he didn't ask if you had a significant woman in your life. Anyone who might serve as a mother to Rex. In spite of some softening toward the end, he rushed to absolve himself of any liability."

"That's okay, Dad."

"Your mom and I can stay a couple of weeks and help you out, but we were gone from our condo a month already. We can't stay at the Lonesome Road indefinitely. And the shape you're still in, how can you take care of your home, the ranch and a baby?"

"My orthopedic doctor said by next week I should be able to shuck the clavicle brace. This troublesome neck collar is going to be part of my life for quite a while. If you and Mom stay long enough to make sure the doctor releases me, I should be okay. JJ's used to covering ranch chores. I have to make it work," he said grimly.

They drove the remainder of the distance in silence. Once home they filled Rio's mother in on all that had transpired. He reiterated his vow to handle everything, including being a single dad.

"I believe you'll try," Linda said without hesitation.

The baby woke up and started to fuss, causing Tag to shake himself out from beneath the hospital bed. The dog raced into Binney's old room and began barking. Tearing out of the bedroom again, he ran around the house alternately barking and whining.

"I think he keeps looking for your nurse," Rob said.

"Oh, so now you can read a dog's mind?" Linda picked up the baby and jiggled Rex. "A week or so of our help won't be enough. Rio, if you can afford it you need to hire a nanny. Which of you wants to hold the baby while I fix his bottle? By the way, did his doctor say when to start cereal? He's a big boy. I don't think this formula is holding him between those listed feeding times someone taped to the cupboard door. Who wrote those? Was it the pediatrician?"

Both Rio and his dad reached out their hands for Rex. Because Linda stood nearer to her husband, she passed the baby to him.

Rio answered her question. "Binney must have taped up the feeding sheet that his aunt left. I think the doctor said to start some kind of cereal, but not right away. She typed findings from her exam and listed information on when to begin his shots. A clerk gave Binney the copy of his record when we checked out."

His mom returned from the kitchen, where she'd warmed the baby's bottle. "Seems to me you relied a lot on her. On your nurse."

"I did." Rio averted his eyes to break his mother's intense scrutiny. "I admit I was clueless. She and Rhonda knew what a baby required and what I needed to buy. Of course, then I didn't expect to keep him. I never would've thought to have Rex seen by a pediatrician the day we went in to have our DNA tested. That was Binney's idea. She knew the midwife who helped deliver Rex probably only gave him a cursory exam."

He let several blank moments tick past then said in a low voice, "On day one when I said I wanted to call social services, Binney swore if she could, she'd apply to adopt him. Then she found the midwife's birth note with my name on it in the tote bag. After that she assumed I was lying about not knowing Lindsey Cooper. But the day we went to get the DNA results, before the tech showed them to us, she said she believed me. Later I screwed up and got all peeved when it seemed she backed Ryder."

Rob stood up. "The baby is wet and smells like maybe he did more than tinkle. I haven't changed a baby in over thirty years, but like they say about never forgetting how to ride a bicycle, I'm sure I can handle this. Where are his diapers, Rio?"

Rio struggled a bit, but got up, too, and hobbled his way into the living room, where he sat heavily in the rocker. "There are packages of diapers stacked under his crib, and a garbage can in the main bathroom that Binney told me should be lined every day with disposable liners and emptied in our Dumpster at the end of the lane."

"Rob, you should let Rio change the baby," his mother called. "If he can't handle that simple chore he'll need to find a nanny right away. Your father and I are only here temporarily," she reminded, framed in the kitchen door, appearing plainly worried.

Rio started to get up out of the rocking chair, but his dad shook his head. Ignoring his wife, Rob completed the task and placed a much happier infant in Rio's lap while he hurried on to the bathroom.

Linda McNabb emerged from the kitchen and passed Rio the bottle. "I'm not being hard-nosed about this to be mean. You're injured and this is a situation of your brother's making. I'm happy to hear you two sort of buried the hatchet. On the other hand he ducked out free again. I wish you'd have demanded some monetary assistance. You shouldn't have to shoulder the entire burden." She reached out and stroked a finger over Rex's dark hair and huffed out a sigh before plopping down in a recliner. "Shoot, it's wrong to imply our first grandchild is a burden. He's sweet as can be. It's you I'm worried about, Rio. But I'd better just shut up."

Rob returned and set both hands on his wife's shoulders. He massaged the back of her neck for a minute, then bent and kissed the top of her head. "Sweetheart, I'm sure Rio knows the origins of your concerns. First reading about his bad accident then walking into this shock after we broke all speed limits to get here caused you a lot of heartache, and that was before we learned what Ryder did."

Setting the partially finished bottle of formula on a side table, Rio lifted Rex and bent him over his broad hand and rubbed his back with the other. "Wearing this cervical collar I can't burp him on my shoulder. Binney showed me this way."

Rex let out one of his loud, classic burps. "See, it works," Rio said grinning at his parents. Tipping the baby back in the crook of his arm, he again offered him the bottle.

"Okay, I'm convinced you aren't completely inept," his mother murmured and smiled.

"Well, there's a world of space between not being inept and being an able-bodied dad. I need both crutches to stand up. I can't do that while holding Rex. I haven't yet showered without some assistance from Binney. She bathed the baby in the kitchen sink in a tub she bought the other night, but I didn't watch. I could probably wash him, but until I'm free of the clavicle brace I probably can't lift him in and out of a tub."

"Don't stress over those things," Rob said, standing between where his wife sat and where Rio still sat rocking the baby. "We're staying until after you have your next doctor's appointment. Your mom can give you tips after you get rid of the brace and crutches. You can carry him around in that front pack. Whoever designed that was genius."

"I still vote for hiring a nanny," Linda stated firmly. She got up and collected the empty bottle, and took it into the kitchen, leaving the men alone.

"I notice every time your mom mentions hiring a nanny you flinch. Why is that? It's pretty plain to me you're going to need help, son. Is it money?"

"No. JJ and I tried to hire a housekeeper for either full- or part-time while I was off at rodeos and he was left to deal with my house, his and the horses. We interviewed a bunch of suitable women, but they all turned down working for us because of how remote the Lonesome Road is. Finally no employment agency in town would send us prospective applicants."

"Hmm. That is a problem. Yet you had a home care nurse."

"Yeah. Binney liked the ranch." Rio left his response at that, but for the remainder of the evening he brooded, wishing he hadn't sent her away. He missed her cheerfulness. He missed watching her blow on Rex's tummy. He missed her joy whenever they trekked out to see Contessa and the other horses.

He knew she had wanted to see the new mare's foal, too. He felt like a damn fool.

OVER THE ENSUING three days he found himself turning, expecting to see Binney anytime the front door opened. Or at night when Rex cried and his mom helped him out of bed to change and feed the baby, he detected Tag searching for Binney. The dog padded to the door of her old room, whimpered and turned accusing eyes on Rio.

It was possible, too, that Rex cried more than usual. Plus, it took longer for the baby and him to go back to sleep in the middle of the night.

MIDMORNING OF DAY four Rio ran across Binney's phone number in his cell phone, and he considered calling her to apologize. He wondered what she was doing. Mostly he worried whether or not she'd gotten another job with some fellow rancher. How often did home health care jobs come up, though? He ought to let her know what all had transpired with Ryder. Would she care that he'd assumed full custody of Rex? He thought she would.

THE NEXT DAY his mom wanted them to go buy a few things at the grocery store. "You need to see if you can handle hauling Rex in the front pack," she said.

He did fine, but women shoppers, even grandmotherly ones, stopped and engaged him in conversation as they cooed over Rex and offered him sympathy.

"Babies attract women of all ages," Linda said

around a grin. "You won't have any problem hiring someone to take care of him. That is, if an agency will send you applicants. Your dad said that was an issue."

Not until after they were in the pickup headed home did he say, "I don't want just anyone to move in and care for Rex, Mom." It was at that moment Rio realized exactly who he did want. *Binney.*

His mother shrugged and dropped the subject while he continued to meditate.

Rob met them outside and helped unload the groceries. Less than an hour later they all sat at the table eating tomato soup and grilled cheese sandwiches. Out of the blue Linda stopped eating and said, "Rio, I knew you'd bought an electronic keyboard and were teaching yourself to play a couple of years ago. When did you take up the guitar?"

"What?" He dropped his soup spoon. "I haven't."

"Then is the guitar case propped against the far end of the baby's crib JJ's or Rhonda's? It's been in the same spot since we got here."

"Huh?" Rio shifted as much in his chair as he could. "Binney plays guitar. Oh, no, she must have forgotten to take it with her when she left."

"Why do you suppose she hasn't called about it?" Linda asked.

"Probably because I acted like a jerk sending her away the way I did." His response sounded stilted.

"Is she the reason you've been moping about for days? I told your dad it's so obvious I've been concerned you may be having second thoughts about keeping Rex."

"I miss Binney," Rio admitted, plucking at his napkin. "I only figured out how much when you drove down the lane from our grocery shopping trip. Binney's the only person I know who could get excited over seeing the sun stream down through the live oak tree branches. She cared about the horses. She weeded your flower beds even though that really wasn't one of her listed duties."

"Do you think her abrupt departure is why Rex and your dog have been extra fretful?"

"I don't know, Mom. Probably. We all depended on Binney. Me most of all if you want the truth. She worked for me, so I kept telling myself not to fall for her. I did and thought it was mutual until we got the baby. For a while that put us at loggerheads. Then we fell into a routine caring for Rex and things picked up again. The DNA results came back. I was steamed at Ryder and got steamed at her for seeming to give him a pass. Remembering what all was said after you guys showed up, I think she maybe just wanted me to calm down."

His mother engaged his father with a quirked eyebrow. "Did you not hear her say before she left that she saw through Ryder, and her concern was for the baby?"

"Yeah, I heard. It didn't fully register because I was so ticked off." Rio ate a few bites of his sandwich, but he struggled to meet his mother's steady gaze.

"I thought maybe you missed her explanation since your dad was phoning Ryder. You handed the nurse her check and told her she didn't have to stay to hear your brother since she'd stick up for him anyway, or something to that effect. To me she sounded sincere when she said after coming here and taking care of you she'd seen through him. I remember it so clearly, because at the time I was totally confused about what the heck was going on."

"I only listened with half an ear. By then Dad had Ryder on the phone. I really, really miss her. I care for her more than a lot."

Rob McNabb, who sat listening to the conversation swirling around the table, squeezed his son's shoulder. "Care for her, or love her? You have that lovesick, sad expression. Hey, I have an idea. Let's let your mother babysit the baby and Tag. I'll fetch that guitar and drive you back into town. You can unburden yourself and beg her to come back."

"I do love her," Rio conceded, sounding awed by his own revelation. "But I screwed everything up, big-time. I was rude. I can't face her, Dad."

"You won't know unless you try. Maybe it's time to cowboy up."

Rio's gaze drifted to Rex, whom his mother had lifted out of his infant seat. "What if she thinks I just need a nanny?"

"You said she was smart," Linda said. "We women can tell when someone is giving us a snow job as opposed to when love is real. Give her credit. Be honest about the hole she's left in your heart."

"I have her phone number. I could just call her."

Linda rolled her eyes. "Phoning, texting, those don't have the same impact."

"You're right. If my name came up in her caller

ID, she probably wouldn't answer. Whether or not she wants to come back I don't want her to go on believing I'm a freakin' toad."

"That's the spirit," his dad said, collecting their dishes and carrying them to the sink.

"Don't think I'm dragging my heels, but I'm not sure where to start hunting for her. Maybe her apartment. I remember the address was on the contract we signed. It's lying on top of the desk in the living room. Dad, it'd be quicker if you go grab it while you pick up the guitar."

"Okay. You head on out to the pickup. Is there anything else you need?"

"Outside of luck being a lady today, nope."

Rio's parents laughed at him, but he didn't think it was so funny. Binney would have every right to toss him out on his rear. He should have told her after they'd kissed that he was falling hard for her. He hadn't given her much to indicate his true feelings.

His dad came out to the pickup carrying an envelope and the guitar. He put Rio's crutches in the backseat and helped him settle in before he climbed behind the wheel and passed him the contract. "Plug that address in your phone GPS, and we'll get this show on the road."

"Thanks." Rio dug out his phone. Within half an hour they sat outside an older apartment building in the heart of Abilene's historic district.

"Her apartment number is three ten. If she lives on the third floor I hope there's an elevator. I haven't tried climbing stairs using crutches. JJ built the ramp for when I relied on a wheelchair. That was all Binney's idea."

"I wondered about that," Rob said. "This building is far from modern. I'd offer to help you, but if it takes effort on your part, son, that will show her you're serious. I'll come into the foyer with you and carry the guitar that far."

Inside it was plain the wide steps leading up were the only means of accessing upper floors. "Showing you have guts is one thing. You shouldn't try navigating stairs carrying a guitar," Rob said, gazing up.

Agreeing, Rio tightened his grip on his crutches. "I'm getting better at using these, and I hope after tomorrow's appointment I'll only need to wear the collar when working out around the ranch. Then I can start building strength and soon I should walk normally."

"I'll take the guitar back to the pickup. Bring her down to get it. I'd like a chance to do more than say hello in passing."

Rio agreed. There was a sturdy handrail and the stairs weren't too steep. He figured out it'd work better if he left one crutch in the lobby and traversed the stairs utilizing the aid of one crutch and the railing. Still he was out of breath when he hobbled to Binney's apartment. Taking a deep breath, he pounded on her door.

And waited.

He knocked again, feeling from the silence it was futile. His heart dived. Her door remained closed, but then the door directly across the hall sprang open. A tiny, very elderly woman peered at him. Rio felt he was being doubly measured.

"Binney's not home. She's at work," the woman said. "You a friend? Or a future client?" she asked, her eyes on his crutch.

"She was working for me until several days ago. I'm Rio McNabb."

"Oh, you're the fella who was injured at the rodeo. Humpf! What do you want? I think you broke her heart."

Rio flinched. "Will you tell me where I can find her if I promise I want to rectify that? By the way, are you the neighbor she plays guitar for? If so, she left her instrument at my ranch. I need to get it back to her. I left it out in my pickup with my dad. I couldn't carry it and climb the stairs."

"Only today did she say she'd left her guitar at your ranch. She's gone back to working full-time at the hospital. In the emergency room. Today her shift is three to eleven, so you've missed her by an hour or so."

"Thanks. Like I said, my dad drove me here. I'll have him swing by the hospital. I hope she won't be too busy to see me." He turned away, walking slowly, guiding himself with his injured hand pressed to the wall.

"You take care. Don't be falling down our stairs. I'm too old and feeble to help you up. And don't you be making Binney cry again or I'll find a way to crack your knees with that crutch."

Stopping at the head of the first set of steps, Rio

laughed. "I believe you will. I swear my intentions are honorable."

His dad was pacing around the lobby. "You didn't call. I couldn't stay double-parked out front. I found a spot down the street. I hate to ask how it went since she hasn't come with you to get her guitar." Rob picked the case up from where he'd propped it against the wall and passed Rio the crutch he'd left in the lobby.

"She's working today at the hospital emergency room. I talked to her feisty neighbor. If I remember right, Binney said the woman is ninety. She threatened to break my kneecaps if I make Binney cry. So I hope our next stop goes well."

"Like I said, you can only do your best. Selfishly I hope it works. Your mother and I have a grandson now, and we always wished for a daughter. The Lord didn't bless us with more than you boys, but maybe He will grace us with a daughter-in-law."

Rio chewed that over as his father went to retrieve the pickup. He hadn't known his folks had wanted more children. Standing there on the sidewalk, he mulled over how nice it'd be to give Rex a brother or sister. And got hot all over picturing him and Binney getting around to that the old-fashioned way.

It was a short drive to the hospital. Rio directed his dad where to park. "I've been here so often now it feels like my home away from home. I even know some of the staff. Surely somebody will help me have a word with Binney."

"Good luck," Rob called after rolling down his window. He gave Rio a thumbs-up.

Unable to stop the smile that spread across his face, he entered through the patient door leading into the emergency room. It seemed a slow day. Several staff dressed in blue scrubs stood around chatting. A couple of them glanced up when the pneumatic door swished open. A tall red-haired woman approached him.

"May we help you? Or direct you to a clinic office?" She eyed his neck collar and his crutches.

"My name is Rio McNabb. I'd like a word with Nurse Binney Taylor. She was my home care nurse for an accident I recently had," he added for good measure. "She, uh, left her guitar at my ranch. I have it out in my pickup. She'll probably want it, but maybe she can walk out with me to get it."

The woman studied him thoroughly as if assessing the validity of his statements.

After some deliberation she said, "Binney's on break. The breakroom is three doors down that hall on your left." She pointed.

"Thank you." Rio shuffled away not nearly as fast as he'd like since he felt all eyes tracking him.

He opened the door, hoping he'd find Binney alone. But no, she sat at a table drinking coffee with four other women all wearing various colors of uniforms. All stopped talking and gave him the same kind of once-over he'd received down the hall. He zeroed in on Binney's lovely face. A face with a glow that made his heart ache.

"Rio!" Binney gaped at him.

He took note of how her hands tightened around her cup.

"I'm here for a couple of reasons. My dad drove me. We…uh…have your guitar in the pickup. You left it at the ranch."

"I only missed it today when my neighbor Mildred asked if I'd play for her sometime this week."

"I met Mildred. She's a pistol. Promised me bodily harm if I make you cry. So please don't."

She frowned slightly and her hands fell to her lap. Rio hurried to fill her in on what she hadn't stayed to hear; his brother admitting Rex was his baby. "He signed over full custody of Rex to me."

She stood then and gripped the back of her chair. "Congratulations on gaining full custody. Are you happy about that?" she asked, hesitantly meeting his eyes.

"I'd be much happier if you'd consent to be my wife and, by virtue of that, Rex's mother. I love you, Binney," he blurted, giving her a lopsided smile. "I don't deserve it, but I hope you can forgive all I said in a fit of anger at Ryder. I've let him get in the way too much in my life. He came to the ranch and we kinda made peace. I regret so badly not taking you at your word when twice you told me you saw through him. I'm sorry." He lifted a hand off one crutch and extended it toward her.

Her mouth had fallen open about the time he said he loved her. Now she cast a hurried glance around at her grinning coworkers. "Talking about Ryder seemed safer than admitting how I was falling for you, Rio. You were my patient. Ryder already meant nothing to me before I spent time with you at the ranch and fell head over heels. Did I hear right? Did you propose to me?"

"I did. I am." It wasn't easy, but Rio tried to bend and kiss her over the cervical collar he still wore. "I don't have a ring to give you. I'll get one. Or you can pick out what you'd like. And we'll have a fancy wedding and invite everyone you want. Really what I want with all my heart is for us to make a family. You, me, Tagalong and Rex, for starters," he said huskily. Then, when most of the women at the table chuckled, he felt himself blush.

Binney rose on tiptoe and kissed him soundly and for so long a cheer went up behind her from her friends. That made her go red in the face, too.

But after she dropped back on her heels, she traced a finger along Rio's jaw. "I don't need a ring. I don't want a fancy wedding. You've offered me what I've most longed for my entire life. A family. To be part of a real family. I accept, Rio. I accept."

Their next kiss blocked out the noise of her co-workers clapping and whistling.

Lifting his lips, Rio said, "Do you have time to go out to the parking lot and say hello to my dad? He felt bad that he never got properly introduced. He said now that he and Mom have a grandson, he hopes they'll soon have a longed-for daughter-in-law."

Binney laughed with joy. Turning to her friends, she said, "You heard. Cover for me until I get back?

It's not every day a woman gets to meet her prospective father-in-law."

"We'll cover," called the woman who'd sat across from Binney. "But only if you promise you'll have a wedding and we're all invited. You've been raving about this guy and his ranch ever since you came back to work. It's only fair that we all get to judge for ourselves. The ranch, that is." The woman winked. "Your cowboy passes muster."

Rio hugged her again, although awkwardly, and laughed a deep, rich sound. "A ranch wedding it is, sweetheart," he said. "You have only to pick a date."

"The sooner, the better." She slid an arm around his waist and moved them toward the door.

* * * * *

If you enjoyed this novel,
look for the next book by Roz Denny Fox,
available from Western Romance in October 2017!

And check out previous books:
HIS RANCH OR HERS
A MAVERICK'S HEART
A MONTANA CHRISTMAS REUNION

MILLS & BOON®

Cherish™

EXPERIENCE THE ULTIMATE RUSH OF FALLING IN LOVE

A sneak peek at next month's titles...

In stores from 15th June 2017:

- **Bound to Her Greek Billionaire** – Rebecca Winters
  and **A Bride, a Barn, and a Baby** –
  Nancy Robards Thompson
- **The Mysterious Italian Houseguest** – Scarlet Wilson
  and **A Second Chance for the Single Dad** –
  Marie Ferrarella

In stores from 29th June 2017:

- **Their Baby Surprise** – Katrina Cudmore
  and **It Started with a Diamond** – Teri Wilson
- **The Marriage of Inconvenience** – Nina Singh
  and **The Maverick Fakes a Bride!** – Christine Rimmer

Just can't wait?
Buy our books online before they hit the shops!
www.millsandboon.co.uk

Also available as eBooks.

MILLS & BOON®

EXCLUSIVE EXTRACT

When Charlotte Aldridge tells CEO Lucian Duval
she's pregnant, the handsome billionaire is adamant
his child will have the one thing he never did – the
love of two committed parents…

Read on for a sneak preview of
THEIR BABY SURPRISE

'I want to be a part of this baby's life on a daily basis.'

The knot of anxiety inside her twisted. 'That's not
possible, you know that, I'm moving away from London.'

'Don't move away.'

Charlotte gestured around her apartment. 'I need more
space. I need to be near my parents. To have family
close by.'

'I agree, that's why I believe you should move in
with me…and for that matter, why we should marry.'

She sank down onto the window seat below the open
window. 'Marry!'

'Yes.'

A known serial dater was proposing marriage. This
was crazy. Lucian had the reputation for being impulsive
and a maverick within the industry but his decisions
were always backed up with sound logic. And that quick-
fire decision making, some would even say recklessness,
often gave him the edge over his more ponderous rivals.
But he had called this one all wrong. She gave an incred-

ulous laugh. 'I bet you don't even believe in marriage?'

He rolled his shoulders and rubbed the back of his neck hard, his expression growing darker before he answered, 'It's the responsible thing to do when a child becomes part of the equation.'

This was crazy. She lifted her hands to her face in shock and exasperation, her hot cheeks burning against the skin of her palms. 'Have you really thought about what it takes to be a father? A child needs consistency, routine, to know that they are the centre of the parent's life. Have you considered the sacrifices needed? Your work life, the constant travel, all of the partying— everything about the way you live now will be affected. Are you prepared to give up all of that?'

Stood in the centre of the room, he folded his arms on his wide imposing chest, his eyes firing with impatient resolve. 'I don't have a choice. This child is my responsibility and duty, I will do whatever it takes to ensure that it has a safe and happy childhood.'

Don't miss
THEIR BABY SURPRISE
by Katrina Cudmore

Available July 2017
www.millsandboon.co.uk